PONGO

HANDS THROUGH THE FOREST

SUE FEENSTRA

Pongo; Hands through the forest
© Sue Feenstra 2018

National Library of Australia Cataloguing-in-Publication entry (pbk)

Author:	Feenstra, Sue, author.
Title:	Pongo; Hands through the forest / Sue Feenstra
ISBN:	978-1-925680-56-0 (paperback)
	978-1-925680-58-4 (ebook)
Subjects:	Fiction -- Environment -- Orangutans
	Fiction -- Forest -- Animals

Published by Sue Feenstra and Ocean Reeve Publishing
www.hellopongo.com
www.oceanreeve.com

REEVE
PUBLISHING

For Will

The story of this spirited young orangutan's adventures
captivated me from the start;
a great read with a real message.
I loved it.

Kobe Steele
Founder and President -
Orangutan Foundation International Australia

Contents

A home like no other

It was a day like any other day in Pongo's rainforest home, laying in his nest, high up in the trees. The young ape curled his waxy brown toes while chewing on some fresh bark his mother had brought him that morning. Unable to sit still, the mischievous youngster writhed around the woody bed, sipping water from a nearby leaf while watching as his mother quietly gathered seeds and fungus nearby; ready for their next meal.

The young ape lived an idyllic life alongside his mother Rangi, far up amongst the treetops on an island called Borneo, where the pair travelled through the woodlands searching for food, water and nests for the night.

Rangi would spend her time teaching her offspring the ways of the forest, how to find food, which fruits you could eat and which you couldn't and where to find water. However, she had learned that lessons needed to be quick and interesting as the lively youngster's attention span could be very short.

The jungle was a magical place; the trees soared up, almost touching the sky and joined together to form arches of green with streams of bright sunlight peeping in between. As far as your eyes could see, moss entwined vines fell from the roof of the forest to the floor down below, alive with activity as birds darted throughout the spaces in between. Pongo would lie in his nest observing the wildlife around him; the butterflies and bees as they buzzed passed him, sometimes landing on his nose to say a quick hello while listening to the sound of nearby hooves crunching over sticks as larger animals moved through the forest floor below, searching for food.

Rangi always told her son that he was very special, but Pongo thought the rainforest was special. It was always so alive, but at the same time such a peaceful place. It was a simple life, but a beautiful one that the young ape cherished.

Leaning out of his nest, Pongo stretched his long orange coloured limb to break off fresh bark. "Mum," he called out, looking down a few branches towards his mother. "You say I am special, but you don't say why?" he asked, twirling the bark through his long toes.

Rangi stopped what she was doing and looked up at her son.

"My darling boy, you are so special, for a start you are my son," Rangi tailed off as she continued to pick at the fungus. "But more than that, you are from a line of Orangutans that are very special." Instantly forgetting the piece of bark, Pongo climbed down a nearby vine to sit alongside his mother.

"But aren't all Orangutans special, Mum?" Pongo asked, picking the fungus his mother had just collected and eating it.

"Pongo," Rangi continued, motioning for him to leave the food alone. "Of course our species is special, but you are Pongo Pygmaeus, your line is very special and very rare my darling son, we must look after you." Rangi paused, retrieving some fungus the youngster was trying to hide. "That is why I must gather food each day to feed you and make you grow and be strong and why I must teach you the ways of the forest," Rangi finished, not sure if her message was being received.

Having already lost interest, the mischievous young ape was now hanging upside down by his feet, alongside his mother, pulling faces as he twirled back and forth.

"But Pongo," his mother continued, looking into his upside-down eyes. "More than anything, you are very special to me," she finished off, handing him back the portion of fungus and tickling his tummy.

Shrieking with laughter, Pongo quickly returned to his nest to while away the rest of the day. Climbing the vine with both fingers and toes the youngster still didn't understand why he was special, or what his mother meant; all that mattered to this playful young ape was that he was special to her.

Rangi looked on, shaking her head and smiling, as her energetic son, rapidly ascended the vine, and without fail completed a final triple somersault to land safely in his nest. *He was naughty,* she thought to herself, *but she loved him.*

The next morning Rangi told her son they were to go down to the water's edge to gather fresh fruits that were growing nearby. Pongo could hardly contain his excitement; he loved travelling to the waters down below. This was a time when other orangutans would meet up and if he was lucky he could share some time with his friends.

Mostly, orangutans lived alone, crisscrossing the forest daily in search of food to feed themselves and their offspring, but every so often they would gather, typically where fruit was plentiful and fresh water was on hand. The younger generation would spend the time chasing each other; tumbling and twirling, burning off copious amounts of energy, while their mothers would gather fruit and share stories, glad of the break from their lively broods.

This day was no different, the climb down was slower than the young ape could manage, because his mother was fully grown and not as agile, but as soon as they were down, Pongo, skipped and rolled all the way to the group of apes that were already assembled.

The youngster loved the waterways and found them enchanting; the break in the trees that followed the brook allowed the sunlight to stream down and touch the water, creating millions of dancing stars, twinkling across its top. It would be easy to sit and gaze at them all day but this young ape had plans. Only once in a while did brook meetings occur and while the mothers would spend the time gathering fruit, the youngsters could catch up and share stories of their own.

First to greet him that morning was another young male, Sabah, who had come from the North East. Sabah was a little older than the younger apes and would willingly use this to his advantage. Pretending to be wiser and know more than the juvenile group, Sabah would trick them into doing stuff that he knew would ultimately get them into trouble.

On one such meeting, the trickster had boasted to the young group that he knew how to swim and could teach them this new skill. Of course the young apes listened, completely mesmerised as he told them of the abundance of fruits and fungus that could be found just across the river.

Now, if you know orangutans, then you know that food is the single most important thing on their mind. As youngsters they need to eat continuously to grow into an adult, and as an adult they need to eat continuously to maintain their large size.

So hearing that there was an area just across the river full of fruits and seeds, was enough for this young group to want to cast all fears aside and find out for themselves.

Sabah's storytelling was compelling as he continued to encourage the youngsters with his inflated yarn until one by one they had all jumped into the brook, completely fearless of the consequences.

Of course, as soon as they hit the fast-flowing water, their infantile bodies began to flay around like rag dolls; the current in the brook catching hold of their small orange frames, throwing them this way and that.

Hearing the shrieks of their offspring turn from fun into fear, the nearby group of mothers stopped what they were doing and raced toward the brook and their terrified broods, passing a remorseless Sabah on route, before finding their youngsters helplessly thrashing about in the water.

One after another, the females retrieved their sodden infants, scolding them at their stupidity and reminding them of how many times they had been told they couldn't swim. On this occasion, Pongo was one of the infants dragged from the water and scolded by his very angry mother.

The young male liked Sabah, although he knew he couldn't trust him. They could have much fun chasing each other through the vines and up the trees, but the energetic youngster was aware that if he were in trouble, it wouldn't be Sabah he could rely on to help him.

Breaking through his thoughts, the juvenile ape heard an excited squeal and turned around to see his best friend, Amelia, running toward him. Her large arms outstretched, she jumped on him and tousled him to the ground.

Rolling around in each other's arms, laughing and screeching, the two continued until they were so out of breath they had to stop, and were content to just lay on their backs and look up at the blue sky.

Amelia was about the same age as Pongo and they had known each other for a few years. An Aunt of his, Aunty Marla, was raising Amelia, but she wasn't her mother.

Rangi told her son previously that Amelia didn't remember what had happened to her own mother, but that she was taken care of by the humans when she was very young. She was given a human name and lived in a place with other young apes where they were cared for and fed by these people.

Each day some of the humans would take a small group of orangutans into the forest where they were allowed to climb and roll and swing while each night they would sleep in a nest that was called a bed. Eventually, the trips to the forest got further and further away, the fences that had stopped the young apes disappearing were gone, and Amelia was allowed to venture alone. Until one day when she returned to the place she'd been brought, finding that her human friends had gone.

Alone and scared, Amelia climbed a vine and perched herself high up in a vacant nest, not sure of what she should do next. Lying on her back in the warmth of the afternoon sun, she watched as the birds darted back and forth, waiting patiently for her human friends to return for her, occasionally looking towards the ground to see if they were there.

But as the afternoon sun shone down on her, the female's eyes grew tired and she began to feel drowsy.

The bark she had been twirling dropped from her fingers and she fell into a deep sleep, lulled by the peaceful chatter of the rainforest.

Not long after, a large female adult orangutan returned to her nest to find a small sleeping infant curled up fast asleep within the bed. Looking over at the young ape she wondered where she had come from, or whom she belonged to? Quickly laying down the food she had gathered, the female looked around her to see if there was anyone about. *Was she to be alarmed that the infant's mother would appear? Should she leave the youngster and find another nest?* The large female ape was very confused.

Marla had lived amongst these particular trees for many years, and knew all of the surrounding families; in fact she had lived alone for several years after losing her own child to a forest fire. Peering into the nest she didn't recognise the infant as one of her friends or that of a nearby ape. Perplexed, the maternal female reached into the nest and touched the sleeping infant's head, a feeling of warmth instantly flowing over her. After a quick look around, she turned back to the nest and sheepishly touched the youngster again, this time a little firmer; the young ape wriggled in response and slowly began to open her eyes. Without warning, an almighty screech broke through the natural buzz of the rainforest as Amelia came face to face with the large female and began to quickly retreat from the nest as fast as she could.

"I'm sorry, I'm sorry," the youngster screeched as she looked for a safe vine to swing to.

Awkwardly, the two apes found themselves grabbing at the same vine, Amelia to escape and Marla to stop her fleeing; the interaction becoming a calamity of entangled orange limbs.

"It's ok, you're alright," Marla's smooth voice interjected. "I'm not going to hurt you, look," she said, pointing at her haul of fruit, fungus and seeds. "Please stay and tell me where you are from?"

Amelia slowly returned to the nest, the draw card of food winning her over, she was starving. Soon the two females were sharing the fruit and swapping stories in the rays of the afternoon sun.

Amelia told the older ape she'd been living in the human place with other orphaned apes and that they'd left her here today, just below this tree; while Marla explained that she'd been alone for many years after losing her child to the fires that swept the forest from time to time.

Marla revealed that she knew something of the humans as she had seen them for many months, sitting and watching her tree. They held something and scraped it with a sharp stick, and put an object up to their eyes when they looked at her nest. At first she was skeptical of them, but they didn't look like they could climb very far or very fast so she was happy for them to be there as long as they didn't disturb her.

The two chatted for some time, while finishing the abundance of food Marla had provided. With their bellies now full, both started to feel drowsy under the glittering lights of the stars.

Instinctively, Amelia felt safe lying next to Marla and soon was sound asleep curled tightly into the female's large fur coated body. Marla couldn't ignore the maternal urges that were beginning to flow through her as she gently stroked the infant's soft coat, before allowing herself to fall asleep alongside her.

The humans only returned one more time; Amelia saw them and they saw her, tumbling about her nest, chewing bark, with Marla just a few branches away collecting food.

Their job here was done; it was clear to see the lone adult female had accepted the orphaned infant, and the young ape had settled into life in the rainforest.

Amelia watched as the humans left; she felt no urge to follow them, even though it would take her straight back to her friends. Here was home now; the forest, the nest, the birds and the stars that twinkled every night, the smell of moss on the ground and the sound of bugs buzzing past your ears, Amelia was happy and so was her Ma.

Pongo and Amelia were now lying on their tummies overlooking the babbling brook, watching as the movement in the water distorted their reflections. The usually coy young male found himself gazing at Amelia's watery likeness, looking at her big brown eyes, and the mop of red hair that fell from her forehead.

For a moment, the young male forgot where he was and without thinking moved his hand towards her reflection and started to trace the outline of her features with his finger.

But as soon as the bashful young ape touched the water, her reflection broke apart, quickly becoming a mass of ripples that extended further and further across the brook. Suddenly, becoming aware of his inappropriate actions, Pongo withdrew his hand from the cool water, hoping his young friend hadn't noticed this unbecoming behaviour.

At the same time and almost as if to save his embarrassment, a fish jumped out of the water right in front of them, splashing the pair before quickly returning to the depths of the brook.

Screeching in response, the two young apes jumped back in surprise and landed firmly on their behinds, the softness of the grass cushioning their infantile frames. The pair remained there for many minutes, laughing uncontrollably as butterflies and bees buzzed passed by them. Pongo lived for these days, but more so he lived for the time he could spend with Amelia.

Suddenly, without warning, their magical moment was broken as Sabah approached with some of the other young apes following closely behind.

"Hey, you two." He walked over and sat down beside the pair, unconcerned as to whether he was disturbing them. "Have you heard what the mothers have been saying about the humans?" he asked the pair, an air of arrogance resonating in his voice.

Both Pongo and Amelia shook their heads in response. "Well," Sabah continued, pitching his voice with an element of fear. "It seems like they are making fires and taking away our forest, many areas have already been destroyed you know," he finished dramatically.

Rolling his eyes in response, Pongo fell backwards and began rocking back and forth, screeching as he clasped his toes in his hands.

"Sabah," he laughed, "another one of your stories!" He rolled around shouting, before eventually returning to a sitting position and shaking his head at Sabah's storytelling. "Why would they do that?" the young ape yelled. "Humans have helped us, look at Amelia, and some of the others." He paused, pointing toward the group that had gathered trying to muster some support. "It's just another story from you Sabah," he finished, looking away from the trickster dismissively.

Sabah stood in response, flaying his long arms up and down and beating his hands on his chest.

"PONGO!" the frustrated ape screeched abruptly. "It's TRUE, I HEARD them, and they were even saying that's why some of our friends are not here today," he continued angrily at the younger ape.

The infantile juveniles behind Sabah nodded as he spoke, hanging on to each word and mimicking Sabah's frustrated body language while Amelia had now jumped back, distressed at the older male's boisterous behaviour.

"Have it your way Pongo," Sabah snapped as he walked away. "You will see," he yelled as he and the group turned toward the woodlands before disappearing amongst some low hanging vines.

Rolling onto his back again, Pongo stared up toward the sky, *Sabah frustrated him,* he thought to himself. *He was always causing trouble and scaring the young apes. It wasn't necessary; here they all were, enjoying the warmth of the day, and the company of their friends and Sabah had to ruin that.* The young ape closed his eyes and let out a large exasperated sigh.

Amelia moved back alongside him and lay down on her tummy, picking at some wild flowers in front of her and eating them one at a time.

"Pongo?" she said softly, gently breaking into his thoughts. "I have heard this myself, from the human place," she confirmed.

Pongo looked in her direction, not wanting to entertain the thought that Sabah might be telling the truth.

"Many of my friends there told stories about the fires," she continued. "And the humans, they, they, sometimes spoke of other humans, not nice like they were, but others, that were destroying the forest with fires," she paused. "I never wanted to say Pongo, because of how Ma lost her son, I didn't think she would want to hear about fires," she finished, her eyes gazing down at the grass with much sadness.

With his day already soured, Pongo decided to stay quiet after this revelation. Even the soothing sound of the forest that usually brought him comfort disappeared, as his mind played host to a million thoughts, as he wondered if there was truth in what Sabah had said.

Soon, their time together ended and the young male prepared to make his way his towards the vines with his mother. It may be some time before he saw Amelia again, and now with stories of fires, he was worried how long that might be. As they parted, he picked a nearby flower and put it in his mouth, not eating it. Pongo took the chance and looked directly into Amelia's eyes; the young female flushed. Fluttering her eyelashes in response, she raised her hand and slowly moved it toward his eye. This gesture could only mean one thing; it was 'I love you' in the language of this gentle species.

As if by magic, the sound of the forest slowly returned to Pongo's senses. The angry thoughts that had been buzzing around his mind all afternoon were gone and all he could hear was the crickets chirping their early evening song and the sound of his joyful heart beating.

As he stood there gazing at his sweet Amelia, drawing a picture of her face in his mind, he wondered when he would see his young friend again. The talks of the fires did concern him and he felt that there may be hard times ahead, but right at this moment, all he knew was complete happiness as he returned to his treetop abode.

Over the following weeks, Rangi reflected on what had been discussed at the last brook meeting and the impact it might have. Of course, there had always been fires in the forest, and she herself had lost friends over the years to them; but this information, if it was true, was different and it worried her.

Natural forest fires could be cruel and you needed to be prepared, but there were characteristics to these fires that the wildlife of the forest relied on.

Typically they were seasonal during which time the creatures of the jungle would know to be on guard. Moreover, they would work together during this time, the birds were the lookouts from the sky, alerting those beneath which way to move to evade the nearing flames while the animals on the ground would keep those above informed as to where the waterways and forest breaks were, providing escape routes for fleeing wildlife.

However, this new information sounded different, the mothers told of fires burning all through the year, and coming from all directions. Rangi was told stories of whole families being trapped, unable to escape ferocious flames. In fact, three families were absent from this brook meeting and the female ape hoped they were all ok and hopefully just displaced.

There was also talk of the intensity of the fires and how strange they were. A true forest fire started small, moving slowly through the undergrowth as it gathered pace. Branches would begin to crackle and a faint smell of smoke would fill the air, giving a subtle warning to the residents of the forest that it was probably time to move. There were also many times a fire simply wouldn't progress at all as it failed to achieve the required elements that were needed for it to develop.

The wind may be too slow, or blowing in the wrong direction, or the rain that drenched the forest most afternoons would dampen the flames, ending the blaze in its tracks.

But these new fires sounded different. They started as giant walls of flames, they needed no wind to carry them and it seemed that no rain was able to stop them. They came from all directions, walls of bright orange flames that soared so high they seemed to kiss the sky. Black smoke swirling around, in all directions, blocking out the sun and turning day into night. Trees that had stood still for hundreds of years simply crumpled and fell to the floor, not able to offer any resistance to the oncoming inferno.

The normal lines of communication failed as anything that got in the way of the fires perished. From the birds who could no longer see the sky through the thick black smoke, to the creatures below who hopelessly tried to out run the giant firestorm that was bearing down on them.

Rangi worried how she would tell her curious young son without scaring him. She needed to protect him, but he was still so young.

The matter was now a topic of daily discussion between Pongo and his mother as he quizzed her about what had been said at the last brook meeting.

Rangi, for the most part, managed to change the subject, deflecting the conversations as they arose but she knew it was just a matter of time before the inquisitive young male asked her again and she would have no choice but to answer his questions sooner or later.

Laying in her nest, her young son sleeping beside her, Rangi debated what she should do. Gently twisting his red hair through her long wax like fingers she gazed into the night sky and silently asked the moon for guidance.

Looking back toward her young son, her worries faded for a moment as she watched him sleeping peacefully. *He looked no bigger than a new baby curled up in the nest,* she thought to herself. Gently stroking his head, the concerned mother decided that tomorrow she would put the call out for a brook meeting. It was an unusual occurrence for this to happen but she thought it was the only way. It was time for the apes to gather, not to pick fruit, or have fun but to come together to discuss the future of the forest.

New Ventures

The forest floor shuddered as truck after truck rolled into the new site, their wheels crunching over the broken branches that had been cleared to allow for easy access. The air was alive with the sound of men yelling at each other along with the noise of heavy engines; both merging together and echoing through the nearby trees, all but drowning out the sound of any wildlife. The smell of diesel began to permeate the air, causing the birds that were sitting high amongst the trees to take flight, unaware that their home and nests were in great danger.

In the distance, a yellow truck carrying two men approached the site and drove toward a small cabin that was positioned off to one side. The vehicle slowed down as it drew closer to the building, finally stopping alongside it. Inside, the two occupants briefly spoke as if arranging a subsequent plan for later; the passenger then leaving the vehicle, slapping the door several times before signalling for it to leave.

The man stood for a minute, surveying the area, while removing his tie in response to the escalating temperature and heat from the nearby trucks. Undoing his top button, he became aware of a male walking toward him and extended his hand to greet him.

"Mr. How?" he smiled toward the man approaching him. "I am Don, Don Henderson, new production manager and owner of Henderson Palm Oil, very pleased to meet you," he said, taking the other man's hand in his own and shaking it firmly.

The small Indonesian man, nodded his head in return and gestured for his guest to enter the cabin. "Come in sir, we are most welcomed to meet you. It is cooler in here, I will fetch you something cold to drink." The two men entered the room, the heat instantly dissipating with the crispness of the air conditioning.

Don Henderson stood and inspected the room, his eyes wandering over the maps that were laid out over two desks, observing the filing cabinets that had seen better days and the air conditioning unit that was supposed to keep them in comfort; if it lasted that long. Breaking into his thoughts, the Indonesian man returned with a glass of cool water. "Here sir," he said, handing him the glass. "We have much work to do," he continued, pointing toward the maps.

With his mouth now refreshed from the water, Don nodded in response. "We do," he agreed. "We certainly do."

Don Henderson was 39 and American, originally from Austin, Texas. He was a tall man, with a mop of dark hair that had shards of silver scattered throughout which glistened in the sunlight. His skin was swarthy brown which had toughened from years living under the harsh South East Asian sun, while his face bore lines around his eyes from continually squinting against the brilliant glare.

Don had spent the last ten years in this region, mainly as a project manager for larger more established Palm oil companies. When his father passed away and left Don a substantial inheritance, he decided to go it alone and start his own company. The savvy businessman intuitively felt that the timing was right. He had two children to think about; Henry, who was six and young Olivia who was just two, as well as his wife Vania, who was herself Indonesian, and whom he had met here.

Walking across the room toward the maps that were laid on the tables, Don stood and studied the grid references that weaved across them. Slowly, he moved his hand over the lines tracing the edge of the forest as the size of his new venture revealed itself to him, causing his mouth to salivate in response. Pausing intermittently, his finger tapped certain positions on the charts as he mentally calculated the scale of the project and the work that would be involved.

Occasionally his gaze would lift and he would stare out of the window that ran alongside him. Looking beyond the men, the trucks and the flurry of activity, he cast his gaze toward the edge of the forest. *This is my forest now,* he thought to himself, *mine and my family's.*

No longer did he have to work for someone else, watching as they reaped the rewards of his hard work. He was his own boss now and the rewards were going to be his.

At that moment Don had an idea and decided that tomorrow he would bring his oldest child, Henry, to the site. It was after all going to be his legacy, so by right, Henry should be involved from day one.

Immediately confirming his intentions, the businessman bellowed across the room at his supervisor. "Mr. How! I will bring my son with me tomorrow!" The small man jumped in response, having been momentarily lost in his own thoughts.

"Of course, sir, this is no problem, how old is your son?" he replied, shuffling papers on his desk, making himself look busy.

"He is six years old," the businessman stated as he turned back toward the window. "Make sure he is looked after, Mr. How," he finished, reaching for some nearby binoculars.

The supervisor sighed under his breath, he knew in his heart that the site was no place for a young child. It was a noisy and dangerous environment. *Nevertheless,* he thought to himself, *he would still have to babysit the son of the new boss if that is what he wanted.*

"No problem sir," he responded politely, "I will organise it right away." He paused. "My name is Bayu,

Sir, you may call me that if you would like." Don turned toward him, lowering his binoculars.

"Bayu, it is then," he replied, nodding toward the man before returning to look out of the window.

Bayu How was a slightly built man with coarse dark hair that was kept closely cropped to accommodate the temperature. Aged only in his mid-twenties, his tarnished leathery skin and lined forehead made him appear somewhat older. Bayu was native to these lands and had grown up amongst the various sites that surrounded this one. As a young boy, he spent his days playing in the forest while his father worked in the nearby fields. Then once he became old enough, he was allowed to work alongside him, slashing the trees before the fires were lit. The job was extremely labour intensive and at a young age, Bayu could see how it affected his father's health. As soon as he was able to, he secured a better job of replanting the cleared sites, making sure his father had a position too.

The young man consciously made a plan that each year he would work hard and prove himself to the bosses so he could get better jobs for them both and

he wouldn't stop until he reached the best position...
supervisor! At that stage he could help his father into
easier roles and look after him.

It had taken him several years and he had learned
many new skills along the way; from driving trucks
to reading site maps but he had done it, he was site
supervisor at 25 years old and was finally able to
give his father the easier job of caretaker of the site
machinery.

Don signalled to his supervisor that they were heading
outside to have a closer inspection of the site. Immediately picking up the binoculars and a rolled-up
map, the two men left the porta-cabin, the heat of the
midday sun hitting them instantly.

The ground was rugged and uneven with the oc-
casional dust swirl blowing up from the hot dry wind
while the pungent smell of smoke and fuel filled the air.

Walking along, the pair passed Bayu's father who
was busy cleaning the body of a large grey truck. The
elderly man looked up towards the two men and

nodded to them respectfully, immediately returning to his work once the pair had passed by.

Nearing the edge of the forest, the heat increased, as did the noise. The men now slashing the undergrowth along with the droning sound of the machinery made it near impossible to hear each other, so the two men resorted to hand signals as a means of communication.

Silently, the swarthy businessman stood and eyed off the area; his eyes fixated on the large expanse of forest in front of him as he quietly congratulated himself on the prosperity this land would bring him. The destruction that was happening in front of his eyes meant nothing, nor did he notice the smouldering ashes that yesterday had been a home to something. No, Don could only see financial success for himself and his family, success that would no doubt come at a huge cost and affect many lives along the way.

The Callout

The rising sun peeked through the branches of the forest, casting a warm light over all that it touched on its journey into the sky. Leaves that had been curled up against the cool of the night unfolded as the orange glow passed over them; while the darkness that covered the forest gradually turned to a brighter hazy green.

With the sun now touching her skin, Rangi knew there was just a short time to put the call out for a meeting before the chatter of the forest grew too loud and drowned out her solitary request.

Sitting up high in her nest, the female ape let out a series of high pitch shrieks; her voice echoing through the trees until fading away in the distance. She paused for a moment, listening out for a response. There was no reply. Once again, she let out a louder call; this time disturbing her sleeping son who was by now sitting up, rubbing his eyes as they adjusted to the morning light. Looking toward the youngster, Rangi gently placed a hand on his shoulder and signalled for him to be quiet. The bewildered young ape was unsure as to why, but followed his mother's instructions nevertheless. Together the pair sat patiently, Rangi letting out intermittent cries in the hope that her message would soon be acknowledged; while her son sat and watched her, hungry but also curious to know what was happening.

Suddenly there was a faint cry somewhere in the distance, almost inaudible above the increasing chatter of the forest, but hopefully returning her call. Quickly turning to face her son, Rangi's eyes widened in anticipation while her heart began to beat faster as she took his hands and listened more carefully. It wasn't long before it came again, this time louder and more distinct, her message had been delivered and her call was being returned.

Soon, the air was alive with the noise of primates carrying the message from tree to tree. Pongo had never heard such a racquet. Standing tall in his nest, holding a nearby vine, he strained as far as he could, to pick out the different sounds, and watched intently as the forest became a flurry of activity. Everything was starting to move. The bark that sat on the side of the tree had come alive as termites scurried along it, while the ground beneath seemed to be moving, like flowing water, as animals ran from every direction.

Sitting in his nest, Pongo's thoughts turned to Amelia and Marla, *What would they be making of this?* He thought to himself. The noise was so loud that even he felt a little scared by it and he wondered if they did too. The young ape took hold of a nearby vine and turned himself upside down, holding on by his feet and slowly beginning to twirl around while searching the forest for any sight or sound of the pair. He let out several small cries before turning his gaze to his mother, realising, a little too late, that he probably should have asked for consent to call out first. Rangi just smiled and repeated his message, knowing her son would be concerned about his friends.

As soon as the sun rose the following day, the excited pair began their journey down toward the brook, his mother explaining firmly that this meeting was not like any other, and he was not to expect to have fun with the other apes. This meeting was to discuss the fires and gather information from all areas before making a plan. Rangi asked her son to look after some of the younger orangutans; giving their mothers time to talk, but she warned him not to go far from the group. This was a meeting where other species might turn up, animals he'd never seen before, some of which could pose a threat.

Pongo listened to his mother and agreed to do as she asked, but really his mind was on Amelia, and how excited he was to see her.

A short time later, the pair arrived at the brook where Pongo was shocked at the sheer number of apes that were arriving for this meeting. As far as his eyes could see, there were mothers with their offspring gathering together, eagerly discussing the danger that threatened their homes. Looking around this vast array, Pongo felt a huge sense of pride. After all it was his mother alone, just one day ago, who put the call out which produced this incredible reaction.

The young ape and his mother moved toward the gathering. Rangi, slowly in her usual cumbersome manner, while her energetic son ran and rolled his way into the group, hurtling along like a bowling ball moving towards a line of skittles. Quickly moving to one side, the older apes parted in response, watching as his tumbling body raced along the soft grass, coming to rest where they had been standing only a moment before. Pongo immediately stood and screeched; hitting his fists on the floor with delight while his mother looked on apologetically, knowing that no matter what the occasion, she was unable to tame his spirited character. The group of apes stayed where they were and watched Pongo's banter before looking up toward Rangi and laughing. She couldn't help but join in with their laughter and shook her head, watching as the youngster entertained them with his finest orangutan gestures.

With his display over, Pongo left the group to their business and proceeded to look for Amelia. Walking alongside the brook he listened for her sound while trying to catch sight of her through these larger than normal crowds.

"She's over there," a familiar voice came from behind him. Pongo turned around to see Sabah standing there with a smug look on his face. "Amelia," the trickster continued, pointing further up the stream. "She's over there with Marla and another group." Pongo acknowledged his help with a polite nod and started walking in the direction Sabah had shown him, pacing himself a little faster, trying to avoid his company. Sabah, however, had every intention of staying alongside him.

"I told you about the fires Pongo, and you wouldn't believe me," the older ape exclaimed. "You think you are better than me, or know more than me," he continued, matching Pongo step for step. "But you're not, you're just a stupid little boy," he ended angrily.

Pongo remained quiet, choosing to ignore the unpleasant comments but his rival continued unabated. "You think you are special and that someone like Amelia will belong to you," he said pointing his finger towards the young ape's chest. "But she won't Pongo, you will see," he finished, laughing at his companion.

Pongo was now furious, and wanted nothing more than to stop and challenge Sabah to a fight; but instead he kept moving, grabbing hold of nearby vines to propel himself faster toward Amelia while hopefully losing Sabah along the way.

By now the journey to find his friend was soured with anger and frustration as Pongo reflected on what the older ape had said. He knew that Sabah had a sweet spot for Amelia, but also knew that he had sweet spots for many other young females whom he would win over with his tales of bravery and courage, most of which were made up.

Endeavouring to push the altercation with Sabah from his mind, the young ape decided not to allow it to ruin another day and the short time he could spend with Amelia.

Finally, a little way further, he caught glimpse of Marla sitting amongst a large group of apes. He exhaled, relieved to know that his young friend would be nearby. Stopping a little short of the group, Pongo looked around him to ensure his rival had departed before continuing toward them and the female that made his heart sing.

Pongo's entrance was greeted by the group with shrieks of delight as his Aunt along with the other females fussed over the arrival of the handsome young male. The young ape grew bashful and stood blushing as they pinched and squeezed him, praising his size and good looks while ruffling his spiky red hair. Although desperately wanting to see Amelia, the embarrassed ape hoped that it would be a few minutes longer, so that she would avoid seeing him being petted like a small boy. It wasn't to be.

The young female popped her head around from behind the group of cooing mothers, giggling at the display they were putting on. Pongo's cheeks reddened even deeper but at the same moment, his heart beat with joy.

Pulling himself free from the clutches of the broody females, Pongo headed toward his friend, laughing with embarrassment at the exhibition that had just been put on, greeting each other with a warm embrace.

With no time to spare, the young male sat down amongst the group and explained that the meeting had been called by his mother, whom was concerned with the fires and the things she had heard. Immediately, the group became restless, each trying to tell their stories at the same time, the shrieks growing louder and louder until not one word was audible.

Pongo raised his hand signalling for quiet. "You must go and find my mother," he instructed the now silent crowd. "We will come and look after the young, but my mother waits, save your stories for then." He finished, with an air of authority resonating in his voice.

The females nodded in response, respectful of his youthful but wise command and immediately began preparing themselves for the journey.

Soon after, the convoy of orangutans was on the move, making its way along the water's edge and up toward the main camp. The journey was going to be slow as the group comprised of all ages and abilities. Some of them were small and agile while there were others that were much older, of great weight or just clumsy. However, they agreed to travel together in order to assist those who were less able and to ensure they all arrived safely.

Marla led the long line of apes as they negotiated their way through the scrubland, leaving Amelia to travel alongside Pongo, at the rear of the group. Walking side by side the two young apes chatted, taking the time to fill each other in on the events that had occurred over the last few weeks. Occasionally, as they sauntered along, their hands would touch, brushing past each other for a brief moment, causing them both to giggle and blush in response.

It wasn't long before Pongo became aware that they had slipped behind the rest of the group who were now several trees ahead. Seizing the opportunity, the love-struck youngster grasped Amelia by the hand and swiftly pulled her from the procession to a nearby clearing. Ignoring the advice his mother had given him earlier; the pair had now become separated from the pack and were completely alone. With little concern, Pongo knew that catching the slow-moving group would be easy. The pair were young and agile, and together they would use the vines and be at the main camp in no time. This was his chance to be alone with Amelia; even if it were for only the briefest of moments, he wasn't going to miss it.

Wulan the Great

The pair of young apes lay on the banks of the brook, staring up at the clouds that bounced along the blue sky above them, watching as they changed shapes before their eyes. The surrounding forest had returned to its natural chatter as the sound of the procession of apes had long since disappeared, leaving them quite alone.

Picking the nearby flowers and eating them, the couple laughed and chatted; occasionally displaying gestures of affection toward each other that were unique to their kind.

The sun was high, but still slightly to the left which gave the pair some shade from the bushes that were growing nearby; while the sound of the babbling brook alongside them produced a continuous murmur that soothed both the mind and the soul.

Pongo's eyes started to grow heavy as the warmth of the sun surrounded him, draining the youngster of any remaining energy.

As he gazed upwards, his eyes followed the line of trees as they danced hypnotically along the edge of the sky, weaving gently back and forth in the breeze.

Finally, unable to resist the urge to sleep anymore, Pongo slowly closed his eyes, letting out a small sigh as he succumbed to the midday siesta.

Amelia was first to wake, unsure if it was the baking sun burning her skin that roused her or if she had indeed heard a noise in the bushes nearby. With her mouth dry, she turned to her mate and gently prodded him awake.

"Pongo," she poked the snoring young ape. "PONGO," she repeated, increasing the tone in her voice. "I heard a noise," she said, trying to moisten her parched lips with her tongue. Pongo promptly woke up to see the sun now sitting on the right side of the centre and beating down on them badly.

"I'm sorry Amelia, what did you say?" he replied shortly, angry with himself for sleeping so long.

"Pongo, I think I heard a sound, over there," she said pointing to the other side of the brook. "I'm sure something has been watching us," she finished fearfully.

Pongo stood and looked in the direction she was pointing to but couldn't see or hear anything, continuing to dust down his sunburned body.

"Come on," he replied, dismissing her fears. "We really must go; my mother and Marla will be so cross," he finished, reaching for her hand and helping to pull her up.

Without any warning, the undergrowth parted across the way and an enormous sound was bestowed upon them, penetrating both of their bodies to the core.

A pair of fierce green eyes appeared and stared at the pair from just meters across what now seemed like a very narrow brook. The creature roared again, its four long yellow teeth bared as it pushed through the bushes, snapping off branches like small twigs, revealing itself to them in all its glory.

With no time to think, Pongo grabbed Amelia's hand and immediately headed toward the nearby vines, grabbing at anything that would lift them both high into the air.

Clutching the first available woody stem, the two apes became airborne as the beast crossed the brook and began chase; its large paws thundering across the forest floor, sending waves of fear through everything it passed. The young pair kept moving as fast as they were able, leaping from one tree to the next as the giant creature with the orange and black stripes continued along underneath them, matching their pace without effort.

Small birds that were sitting nearby lifted swiftly into the air as the beast raced by them, avoiding being caught up in a pursuit not intended for them. At the same time creatures that lived in the burrows beneath rounded up their offspring and quickly disappeared beneath the earth's surface, waiting for the danger to pass.

Amelia's heart was pounding so hard that her whole body shook and her hands had become clammy with fear. The sun rash that had bothered the couple just a few moments ago was instantly forgotten as they raced through the trees, trying to outrun this creature, which had the young pair in its sights.

Amidst the panic, Amelia lost her grip and began to tumble backwards, crashing through the leaves and branches as she fell towards the ground below. Disorientated and desperate, she stretched out her long brown fingers and tried to grab hold of anything that would break her fall and prevent the certain fate which waited beneath.

Her screams of fear echoed through the jungle, stopping Pongo in his tracks. He turned in response to check that his young friend was still alongside him. She wasn't. Looking around, his heart racing, he realised that Amelia was now several trees behind him, barely clutching a branch just meters off the ground, screaming as the tiger loomed closer to her. Quickly doubling back, Pongo began swinging through the trees which he had just cleared, hoping he could reach his friend before it was too late.

Amelia was exhausted, her hands were tired and sore and her body was caught up in a mixture of leaves, branches and old vines that had gathered over time in the nook of the tree. She was stuck, with only the remaining strength in her fingers preventing certain death.

By now the striped beast had also been alerted by the screams, immediately slowing down in response, his attention now focused on the area the panicked sound was coming from. Moving slowly, his muscles rippling as he proceeded through the undergrowth, the majestic animal crept along, his eyes fixated on his prey.

Pongo was all but two vines away when he saw the tiger approaching the tree where his young friend was stuck. He watched as the beast narrowed its feline eyes, lowered his body and began swishing his tail. *There was no time,* he thought to himself, *the beast was about to attack.*

Moving stealth like through the branches, Pongo travelled through the trees until he was directly above his young friend, hopefully able to reach her before it was too late. Amelia caught his eye as he motioned for her to reach for his hand when he signalled; he would then pull her free and release her from her woody trap.

Turning himself upside down, Pongo wrapped his wax like toes around a strong vine and began lowering his body towards his friend, keeping his eyes fixed on the beast; careful not to break the gaze the animal had on Amelia, aware he could prompt it to react sooner.

Amelia could now smell the beast as it approached her and hear its throaty purr. Slowly it crept closer, until the moment where there was no more noise, no screaming and no movement, just a complete standoff between these three creatures in the middle of a deserted forest.

First to move was Pongo, quickly extending his hand down and lengthening his long waxy fingers as far as he could to provide a better grip to his friend. Amelia immediately let go of the branch she had been holding and reached up, her hand soon encompassed by his as he started to pull her out from the nest. At the same time, the tiger snarled and pounced, its feet hitting the side of the tree, sending shudders through each and every branch. Its muscular body covered a third of the height of the trunk, bringing it closer to Amelia's tiny body. Tightening his grip, Pongo used his spare hand to hold a higher branch to help leverage her out of the trap, and began pulling with all his might.

All Amelia could feel as her body broke free, was the warm breath of the beast as its jaws slammed shut behind her; tearing at her fur as she was propelled from the trap upwards towards the higher vines. Tightening his grip around Amelia's hand, Pongo hurled her body upwards and away from danger, his feet still firmly grasping the branch above, swinging them both out of reach of the beast.

With a loud thud, the tiger lowered himself from the tree, his paws thumping on the ground as he landed beneath, utterly dismayed his meal for the day was gone.

Still high with adrenalin, Wulan the Great paced back and forth beneath the tree for some time, growling intermittently, hoping that his luck might change and an exhausted ape may still drop into his lap. Eventually though as the thrill of the chase subsided, boredom and embarrassment took its place, and the majestic creature sauntered off into the jungle, his golden stripes glistening in the afternoon sun as his throaty purr faded into the everyday sound of the forest.

Pongo and Amelia sat amongst the treetops for some time in silence, their chests were heavy with breath and their minds still full of fear. Amelia's body, both terrified and exhausted, would intermittently shudder as the shock of what just happened took hold, while Pongo sat with his head hung low; he was both relieved at their escape but at the same time ashamed that he had brought about this situation.

As the night drew in, neither ape had moved from the treetop they had found. They had both heard the beast wander off some time ago, but were too tired and too scared to try and find a better nest for the night.

Lost and alone, the exhausted male pulled at some branches from nearby trees and made a small bed for Amelia, laying some leaves across it and motioning for her to lie down.

Looking at his friend as she curled her small body up against the coolness of the night, Pongo's thoughts turned to Marla and his mother, knowing they would both be furious and scared for the pair. Berating himself the young ape shook his head as he desperately tried to spot anything around him that was familiar; but nothing was, tonight not even the stars in the sky were able to guide them home.

Maybe Sabah was right and he would never win Amelia's heart, the dismayed ape thought angrily. *Maybe he was after all just a stupid little boy*, he sighed heavily under his breath.

As the youngster watched Amelia sleeping, Pongo decided that he needed sleep too. Chastising himself tonight was not going to help them, no matter how badly he felt.

Moving from his tree, the ape quietly stepped on to the makeshift nest to lie alongside Amelia, trying his hardest not to disturb her. They were quite high up where the breeze was cooler, so Pongo curled into his friend and wrapped his long orange arm around her, sheltering her from the night air while lifting his fur covered leg over hers to keep both of their bodies warm through the hours that lay ahead.

The day had not gone to plan at all, and as the young male ape started to drift off to sleep, his mind wandered over all the things that had occurred, from the moment he left the safety of his mother's nest that morning to saving Amelia from the jaws of the giant beast. Shuffling his body closer to his friend, Pongo closed his eyes and hoped that tomorrow would be a better day and that the young pair would find their way back to the safety of their families without any further events.

Cease ignition

Bayu did not hear the sound of the black car approaching the porta-cabin that morning, as the noise of the nearby machinery drowned out the sound of the engine. Rather, it was the dust swirl that billowed from the vehicle's rear tyres that caught his eye, causing him to notice the car's arrival. Quickly leaving what he was doing, the young supervisor rushed toward the cabin to greet his new boss who was here today with his son, Henry, a young boy of six years old.

The car drew to a standstill just short of the building, a swirl of dust filling the space around the vehicle before dispersing swiftly into the atmosphere. The driver's door opened and a Caucasian man appeared, wearing a dark suit, and proceeded to walk around the car. Bayu nodded as the man passed him, but received no acknowledgment in return. The man just continued to the back door of the car in a robotic manner and opened it without making a sound.

First out of the vehicle was Don Henderson, still in a shirt and tie and still undoing it upon exit as the heat of the site took hold. Next was a small Indonesian boy, who hopped out behind Don, gasping in awe at the size of the work site.

Confused, Bayu leaned down to look beyond the boy into the rear of the car ready for another child to emerge.

Was he to care for two children today? Had Henry brought a playmate, he worried as he looked into the back of the vehicle, searching for the second child. However, his fears were soon eased as Don introduced the small boy. "Mr. How...., sorry," he stumbled, before correcting himself. "Bayu," he paused and turned to the child. "This is my son, Henry," he said, pointing toward the young Indonesian boy. "Henry, this is Bayu, Bayu works for me," he said, repeating the greeting to his young son. Henry stopped twirling around and extended his small olive coloured hand towards the supervisor who took it in his own and shook it.

"Will that be all?" a voice interrupted from behind them. Don promptly turned to acknowledge the driver's question.

"Yes, Frank, yes, that is all, return quickly to Vania and you can help her once the nanny has arrived for Olivia," he replied, dismissing his driver with little flicks of his hand while tugging at his uncomfortable tie with the other. The driver obediently got into the car and quickly drove away, the plume of dust once again swirling behind him as he left the site.

The two men and small boy quickly moved toward the porta-cabin, Bayu standing back and holding the door open, allowing his boss and his son to enter first.

Once inside, Bayu got two bottles of water from the nearby fridge and handed one to Don and one to his son. Don snapped the lid open, promptly walking toward the window to survey the site. Henry smiled in response, acknowledging the gesture to the young supervisor.

Henry was a slightly built boy, with an accent that encompassed his father's American tone with some Indonesian undertones. He had very little in the way of his father's looks and Bayu now presumed that he must take after his mother, who would obviously be Indonesian. However, the young boy looked every part of Bayu's culture and if it wasn't for his neatly pressed blue shorts and crisp white shirt, he could be the son of any of his workers, including himself.

The irony wasn't lost on Bayu, as he looked out from the window of the cabin to see his own father, at nearly 60 years old, cleaning the wheels of a nearby truck; his body bent over and tired and his skin parched from decades of harsh South East Asian sun.

We are all dealt our own hand, Bayu quietly thought to himself, shaking his head as he collected the empty water bottle his boss had carelessly discarded on a nearby desk.

The day ahead would be busy. Bayu was to ensure that Henry was looked after and enjoyed his time at the site, but also that the daily operations ran smoothly; something that was time consuming and required his full attention. However, there WAS something about this young boy that Bayu liked, that reminded him of himself when he was a child. Beneath the formal attire was a youngster that was both inquisitive and sensitive, a child that wanted to know more than whether this was his father's legacy. Rather, he wanted to know about the land and the people, asking question upon question that at times, Bayu had difficulty keeping up.

By now Henry's shorts had become a mixture of navy cotton and brown dust and his shirt all crumpled and grubby, as he hurtled from one area to the other, learning as much as he could while his father stood nearby at the edge of the forest surveying the area and oblivious to his son's energetic activities.

By noon, the youngster had met most of the workers and was now sitting alongside Bayu's father, on the floor, asking him questions about the trucks while sharing some well-deserved water with him.

Apart from the presence of the spirited young guest, the day was turning out to be like any other. The trucks moved back and forth, collecting the debris the fires left behind while workers slashed new areas, clearing what seemed like football fields at a time. A constant stream of birds circled the skies above as one by one their homes were slashed or burned from existence while men with wheelbarrows removed wildlife that had not been lucky enough to escape the blazing infernos.

The noise of the site was a mixture of all sounds, which blended into a horrible commotion as men yelled, machinery whirred and birds screeched. The smell was a concoction of smoke, fuel and freshly cut foliage. The environment was not pleasant. It was hot, it was hard and the cruelty of the situation was easily forgotten to the pay cheques that kept these workers employed and their own families fed.

Bayu was keeping up with the pace of the day, dividing his time between his daily workload along with looking after his lively young friend who was now sitting back alongside Wayan, Bayu's father, creating patterns in the sand with a long stick. Suddenly a gust of wind prompted Bayu to look up from the young boy, his eyes catching unusual movements in the tree line. The supervisor looked around anxiously before turning toward the forecourt and looking toward the ground. The dust swirls on the floor usually danced in harmony, twisting and turning together as if performing some sand like waltz; the direction of which would inform which way the wind was blowing. But at this moment Bayu saw no unison. Instead the swirls moved against each other and against themselves, twisting one way and then the other. The small clouds of dust fought desperately against the gusts of wind that were stirring them up. Turning his head back to the tree line, Bayu could see the trees, moving erratically, back and forth and side to side as they too succumbed to the sudden change in atmosphere.

Bayu nervously ran his hands through his hair and moistened his index finger, holding it up to the oncoming wind. The result wasn't good, the wind was changing direction, and changing quickly. This would affect the direction of the fires, possibly driving it toward them, or in a direction that affected land that was not theirs.

Quickly the young supervisor started to run towards the line of workers that were in charge of lighting the fuel. Waving his hands, he yelled as loud as he was able, trying to attract the attention of the foreman, desperate for him not to ignite anything else. Using his radio, Bayu issued instructions, "Cease ignition, cease ignition!" but as he moved toward them, he could see the foreman did not reach for his own radio in response; the noise of the site drowning out any crackly requests.

Noticing the supervisor running toward the fire line, Don quickly joined him in pursuit, having also becoming aware of the changing climate himself. "Darn it," he muttered underneath his breath, this was a drama he did not need at this early stage.

As quick as they were able, Bayu and Don approached the fire line. The heat of the infernos slowing both down as they moved closer. The ground beneath them was uneven; a mixture of soil, rocks and old tree stumps, causing both men to constantly look down to prevent falling. Regardless, Bayu continued to shout, "Cease ignition, cease ignition!" in the hope new fires weren't lit. It wasn't to be.

About 100 metres from the area, they watched as three men approached a fresh line of slashed trees and threw their torches deep into the foliage. Standing back, the workers cheered as a giant fireball ignited, sending a plume of black smoke billowing into the sky, the smell of burning fuel instantly filling their nostrils and the air that surrounded them. Choking back the stench, Bayu continued toward them, waving his arms and shouting for them to stop, as a further three torches entered another section of trees and more fire began curling into the smoky black sky.

Usually the crackling and ferocity of the flames could almost drown out the sound of men hollering, but this time even the noise of the fire couldn't mask the sound of fear and pain as the swirling fire changed direction, circling the ground the workers were just standing on.

With a blue orange flame, the fire licked at the low-lying foliage, tracing the areas where fuel had mistakenly fallen and wrapping around the men's feet as they tried to outrun the raging inferno. Thinking quickly, Bayu changed his commands into his radio, calling for the water truck, the medical truck, and all hands to come and help. He observed his workers fleeing from the area, their legs and lower bodies charred and burned while the fire behind them continued in a completely new direction.

The area soon became a hive of activity as workers approached from everywhere. The water truck headed immediately into the forest and began dousing the flames that were by now burning out of control, while men tended the injured, cutting away their shorts and treating their wounds onsite before organising for them to be evacuated to a nearby medical facility. Don was by now bare chested, using his shirt and tie as tourniquets or dressings while Bayu was organising emergency transportation for the injured men as well as instructing the water trucks where to douse next.

The next several hours were chaos as men arrived from everywhere, trying to help as much as they could, including Bayu's father who had left the truck he was cleaning to offer assistance in whatever way he was able. Eventually though as the majority of the fires were extinguished and the injured men evacuated, the site resumed its pace, albeit more sombre and with everyone a little more exhausted.

Walking over to his boss, the thirsty supervisor accepted the bottle of water on offer, thanking him before raising it to his dry mouth, and drinking heavily from its contents. The two men stood for a minute, silently observing the area, and contemplating the damage, momentarily shaking their heads as they took it all in. A fire WAS still burning, but it was within their boundaries and it could be monitored over the remainder of the day, while the injured workers appeared to have received only superficial burns and would be back at work within weeks. Bayu had excelled in his job, limiting what could have potentially been a very nasty situation. Don recognised this and respected the young man's abilities.

With the site under control both men turned and left, Don patting his supervisor on the back in appreciation as they headed back toward the porta-cabin.

It had been sometime since the event unfolded and as they walked, Don's thoughts turned to Henry who would by now be bored or tired and definitely in need of food. Exhausted by the events, Don made the decision that on their return he would call his driver to immediately take both he and his son home.

A few minutes later the men walked passed the truck that Bayu's father had been cleaning before the fire broke out, which was standing alone awaiting the return of the elderly man.

Passing the vehicle, the men headed toward the building, dusting themselves off before they entered. The crisp cool breeze from the running air conditioner instantly hit the men, the fresh air embracing their hot bare limbs, providing instant relief to their tired bodies.

"Henry!" Don shouted as he moved towards the fridge and reached for two bottles of water. "Henry!" he shouted a little louder, turning and looking around the room. Taking the fresh bottle of water from his boss, Bayu started undoing the top while walking across the room toward the desk. "Henry!" he called out, as he approached the messy work station.

Both men looked at each other, concern now growing that their calls were being met with a deafening silence. Casting his mind back to when he had last seen the boy, the supervisor recalled seeing Henry with his father by the truck. Quickly he raced out to the unattended vehicle, hoping that Henry was inside, possibly asleep. However, it was not to be, the truck was empty and offered no clue on where the small boy might be.

Immediately discarding his water, the supervisor began running toward the scene of the fire, shouting for his father as he hurtled across the rough terrain. Don, who was by now starting to panic stayed behind, calling out his son's name while hurriedly moving from one location to another.

"Check the other vehicles Don!" Bayu yelled back to his boss, pointing at several trucks that sat alongside the cabin. "He could be in one of those," he continued as he sprinted further away.

The anxious father moved quickly to the area his supervisor had identified, calling for his son as he scrambled amongst the bodies of the vehicles, hoping to find him hidden in one. "He's only six," the man cried out toward some passing workers. "I left him in your care," he continued angrily, asserting his frustration.

Nearby, Wayan became aware of the commotion and quickly hurried to the edge of the clearing to see what was going on. "Father," Bayu gasped as he arrived alongside him. "Father, where is Henry?" He paused, placing his hand on his knees as he caught his breath. "He was with you, by the truck, before the fire," he finished, still breathing heavily. Wayan moved to the front of the group that was gathering.

"Bayu, he was playing in the grass, alongside me, then there was a call," he paused, looking back toward the cabin. "There was a call for all help and I quickly came," Wayan answered, unsure as to what had happened. "Bayu, I am sorry, I just don't know," the elderly man confessed as he looked toward the rest of the men.

Straightening himself up, Bayu ran his hands through his hair, his lips pursed and nostrils flaring as he inhaled big deep breaths and tried to form a plan in his mind.

"Ok, ok," he replied anxiously, nodding his head. "Ok, where, where did you see him last?" he asked his father. "Anyone, anyone, did you see the small boy?" he extended the question to the group, who collectively shook their heads in response, while his father could only point to the grass section nearest to the truck.

"Ok," Bayu said. "You, you and you," he said pointing at three of the group. "And you Father, come with me now. The rest of you, keep dousing the flames and if you see or hear the boy, radio me immediately!" he said, as he left the area.

Quickly arriving back at the vehicle, the group of men was met by the anxious American who was continuing his own search for the small boy. Frantically Don ran from one place to another, calling his son's name over and over, repeating his accusations as to who was to blame for the situation.

"Don, over here!" Bayu shouted and waved to his boss, doing his best to ignore the man's accusations. "Wayan saw Henry playing here just before the fire broke out," he continued, moving toward the edge of the scrubland.

Leaving the trucks, Don ran over to the grassy area, still frantically calling the young child's name and yelling at anyone he passed on route.

The fast thinking supervisor quickly raised his arm as the tall man approached, blocking him from entering the area in an attempt to protect any evidence that may be there.

Immediately the workers started searching the area, soon noticing a trail of flattened grass and broken sticks, a strong indication that the boy had indeed been here. Continuing to follow the track, it soon became evident to the group that Henry, for whatever reason, had travelled away from the site and in the direction of the forest.

While the men continued to track the path that led toward the trees ahead, Bayu stood and looked beyond them, fear steadily growing from the pit of his stomach, knowing this situation was not good at all.

Aside from the normal dangers that the forest presented, there was now also the out of control fire to consider and at that moment the worried supervisor knew that Henry was out there, alone and in great danger.

Chasing Lizards

Henry had been lying in the cool grass with the heat of the afternoon sun beating on his back. The old man near the truck was at the far side of the vehicle, leaving the young boy to his own adventures.

In the distance, Henry could hear men shouting and machinery moving, but right at that moment it was just himself and the lizards playing amongst the tall wispy grass.

The young boy carefully broke the small branches off a stick and crawled on his belly in search of new friends to play with. It wasn't long before a small lizard appeared, sun bathing on top of a warm rock. With its neon green scaly skin and frilly neck collar, the lizard would easily blend amongst the reeds of grass. But when sat on top of the blackened rock, it had no disguise and the young boy quietly wriggled toward it.

Henry was now within a meter of the bright green reptile and could see its bulbous eyes darting, independent of each other, scanning for nearby danger, while its rounded body expanded with each breath it took.

Wriggling closer still, the young boy slowly raised a stick toward his scaly friend who let out a series of clicking sounds in response, before darting off behind the rock. Dropping the stick in response, Henry continued on his tummy, crawling across the undergrowth in pursuit of his friend as the game of cat and mouse unfolded.

Scrambling through bushes, Henry and the lizard moved as fast as each other, stopping intermittently to perform a Mexican stand-off, staring each other down before one of them made the first move and the chase began again.

Soon other lizards joined in the game and Henry found himself chasing this way and that, trying his hardest to reach out and grab one. There was so much fun to be had that the young boy didn't notice that the grass around him was now much thicker and the sun that had been beating on his back was now hidden behind the trees that soared above him. He also paid no attention to the fact that the lizards he was chasing had changed colour, from a bright luminous green to a deeper more olive colour in keeping with the denser surroundings.

Oblivious to these changes, Henry continued his pursuit, convinced he would capture at least one of these creatures before it was time to go home.

Without warning the lizards that had been teasing him all afternoon scampered away, leaving the young boy standing amongst the thick grass alone. Turning around, Henry searched the area for more scaly reptiles to play with, before becoming aware that he no longer knew where he was. Surrounded by tall leafy plants, the young boy stopped to listen out for the noise of the nearby trucks or men yelling for guidance, but there was none. The natural buzz of the forest had drowned out any sound that his kind could generate, leaving him completely lost and alone in the forest.

And then there were three

Pongo was first to open his eyes the following morning as the warmth of the sun touched his body, gently waking him from his sleep. Startled, he looked at Amelia lying alongside him as the memories from the day before returned to his mind; the feeling of guilt and shame following soon after.

Within a few moments, his young friend began to stir also as the noise of the surrounding area grew and the sun continued its journey into the sky; stretching her smaller frame in response as the warm rays passed over her aching body.

Without speaking, the two young apes sat in silence for a while, as feelings from the day before came flooding back, bringing with it an awkwardness the pair had never before encountered.

Deciding to cast the tension aside, Pongo began to talk, revealing a plan that he was sure would lead them both back home. Using the sun as a guide, he explained that the pair would follow its path across the sky, using the shadows from their bodies on the trees to steer them in the right direction. But, before anything could begin they needed food, so tugging at some nearby trunks, the young male started peeling back chunks of termite ridden bark and offering them to his friend for them both to pick at. With their bellies still empty from the day before, the pair began hastily devouring some fungus that they had spotted nearby along with some low hanging leaves that held fresh water from the night before.

Soon both apes had consumed enough food and water to embark on the journey ahead and leaving the safety of the nest, the two apes began to propel themselves gracefully through the branches and closer to home.

Not too much time had passed before Pongo sensed they were not alone, the sound of the vines creaking with movements nearby indicated there was another creature close by to them. *Hopefully someone who could help guide them correctly back to the brook*, thought Pongo.

Signalling for Amelia to stop, the young male listened out for movement other than their own. There was nothing, but still the young ape sensed something WAS there and decided they should change directions and take a look.

Occasionally the young male stopped and peeked through the trees, trying to spot another ape before continuing slowly and cautiously through the vines.

Suddenly he caught glimpse of some red fur and long waxy fingers curled around a nearby trunk and he quickly moved toward it, signalling for Amelia to stay put. Picking up speed, the young ape moved swiftly from one vine to the next, observing the distinctive outline of another ape, now moving away from him and for whatever reason, trying to avoid him.

Changing direction, Pongo knew he could use the vines to his advantage, by utilising both his fingers and toes he could quickly manoeuvre through the trees and double his speed, cutting the ape off up ahead.

In no time at all Pongo was in front of the suspicious animal and waiting for him to swing toward him, probably unaware he had even been out manoeuvred. As expected, the mysterious ape soon appeared and Pongo could not have been more surprised.

"Sabah!" Pongo shouted in shock as the mischievous ape landed in the tree alongside him. Sabah stuttered and stammered a greeting, trying to avoid any eye contact and seemingly ready and eager to continue his journey.

"Sabah!" Pongo continued with an undertone of frustration. "What are you doing here? Where are we? Are we near the brook?" he continued, a million questions running through his mind. Sabah muttered a few obscure sentences and again tried to move to a new vine, keen to carry on his journey.

"SABAH!!" Pongo yelled as his frustration gave way to anger. "You've always got something to say, so answer me. Amelia is over there waiting, we got lost, where are we?" he asked again, as Sabah began to release his grip on the vine and relax.

"I don't know Pongo, I'm lost too," the conniving ape finally replied as he began looking through the trees in Amelia's direction. Feeling irritated with the vague response, the younger male turned and signalled for Amelia to join them; knowing that regardless of his rival's inability to explain his circumstances, they would be safer as a group.

Once together, Sabah reluctantly opened up a bit more, explaining that he too had become separated from the group and lost his way. Revealing, that he didn't have any idea as to where they were or how far from the brook they were, all he could say was that he fell behind the group and had gotten lost.

Pongo was suspicious of his story, but decided to let it go for now knowing there would be a better time to find out just how Sabah came to be at the same place as the two of them. But for now, it was a good time to rest and take advantage of some fresh bark and fungus, before continuing the journey using their shadows to guide them along.

The remainder of the day was uneventful with the three apes moving through the trees, looking and listening for anything of significance that they recognised until finally the sun started to drop behind them and they found themselves still nowhere nearer to home.

Eventually, as the sun finally disappeared from the sky and the chill from the night air was beginning to take hold, the trio stopped to find nests and make beds that would be safe for the night. Feeling downcast, Pongo could not even believe he was here; hungry, lost and alone, not only with Amelia but now Sabah too.

Quietly, in the security of his bed, he gently shook his head to himself. He missed his mother so much, he missed her warm touch and he began to wonder if he'd ever see her again. The young ape's brown eyes became watery at the thought and he quickly turned away from the other two, not wanting them to see the tears that were now rolling over his rounded cheeks. Closing his eyes, he began to fall asleep under the blanket of stars that he loved so much. Keeping the thought of his mother foremost in his heart and mind, the young ape fell asleep dreaming of his green leafy home.

It was the squeals of Amelia's laughter that woke Pongo from his night's sleep. Rubbing his eyes and looking across from his nest, he could see the two apes sat together across from him; Amelia laughing at the tales the older male was telling her.

Sitting up in response, Pongo's cheeks began to flush as feelings of rage and jealousy surged through him, annoyed with himself that he had not woken sooner.

Quickly reaching for some nearby vines, the young male manoeuvred closer to the pair, tearing at some bark along the way and hoovering up the termites as he negotiated his way through the trees.

Oblivious to his arrival, Amelia continued to squeal and giggle at Sabah's stories, occasionally rolling backward in her nest, reaching for her toes with her long waxy fingers, seemingly in fits of laughter. Feeling like the outsider, Pongo entered the nest with a certain amount of trepidation as the two apes continued their raucous banter without him.

"Well Pongo, which way today?" Sabah said sarcastically as he handed Amelia some fresh fungus he'd pulled from a nearby tree.

"I'm not sure," Pongo replied solemnly. "Maybe we should all decide," he offered, not wanting to take the responsibility of sole decision maker.

Sabah rolled onto his side and extended his long red limb to pick at more fungus for himself and Amelia.

"Well," he continued chewing on his spongy meal. "As long as we don't head back to where that tiger was, he was big!" he exclaimed, his eyes widening. "Like, when I saw him grab at your leg," he continued, pointing to Amelia. "I thought you were a goner."

Pongo tilted his head. "You saw that creature?" he asked, perplexed as to what Sabah had said. "You were there?" he asked again, trying to understand just how he could have seen it.

The older ape quickly jumped up and extended both of his arms to take hold of a nearby branch. "We must head that way I think," he replied, hastily changing the subject and pointing randomly into the forest with his foot. "Yep," he continued. "That way, come on Amelia," he commanded, reaching down with his hand to help pull the young female up.

Pongo fell in line and followed the pair as they started moving through the trees, but his mind was now pre-occupied as to what Sabah had just revealed. As he started the day's journey, his brain would not let it go.

Gliding through the vines, the young ape could not help but go over the moment the creature had leapt from the bushes. *Had Sabah been there too at that moment?* he thought to himself.

Stretching his long arms out, grasping one woody stem after another, the confused ape tried to work out the timeline from the incident at the brook to when Amelia was nearly bitten by the tiger; leaving him to wonder if Sabah had been there the whole time?

Something didn't add up and Pongo wanted to get to the bottom of it. His older rival was hiding something and he would have to find out what.

Amelia's squeal broke through Pongo's thoughts and he looked over toward his young friend to see her quickly descending through the branches, heading toward something below that he'd never seen before.

"My human place!" Amelia declared loudly, pointing toward some abandoned buildings. "It's my human place!" she shouted, turning to her companions and smiling as she continued down through the branches to the structures beneath.

Cautiously, the two males lowered themselves onto a platform and stood observing their surroundings. Amelia skipped, rolled and jumped from one area to another, pointing excitedly toward things, explaining to her two friends what they were.

Pongo had never seen anything like it, funny shaped houses made from wood that were surrounded by still green water. Slowly he looked around, taking in what had once been Amelia's home and home to many others of his kind. But not now. There was no one here, for whatever reason, the place had been abandoned.

The rest of the day was spent with Amelia showing her friends what the humans used to do here, the tools they used to build things and chairs they used to sit on while feeding the infants. The two males laughed as Amelia pretended to be a human, washing herself in the water and eating food using some strange shaped objects. Finally they all sat together peacefully on the platform, listening to the sound of the forest.

At that time and with the mood a little lighter, a decision was made between them to stay here for a day or two. It seemed safe and provided good shelter. Nearby there was an abundance of food as the humans had planted trees that were now heavily laden with fruit. Mostly, they hoped that in time, Amelia could remember some of the walks into the forest she took that led her to Ma's nest, which would hopefully bring them closer to their own homes.

Sabah stood and offered to go alone and gather food for them all. It was a gracious gesture, but not given without reason. The devious male was more than happy to sit and pick food for the others while devouring as much as he could on his own. Considering himself the largest of the three, he willingly gave himself permission to do so, *They may need his strength at some point, and as a result he should be entitled to eat more.* Watching as he left for the orchard, Pongo and Amelia sat quietly on the platform, observing the wildlife around them, the young female occasionally pointing to things and explaining their significance to her friend.

The pair had spent no time together since Sabah joined them and Pongo decided to seize the moment and discuss the things that were troubling him.

Moving closer to the female ape, the confused young male began to talk.

"Did you hear what Sabah said about that creature?" he quietly asked, while shifting his feet so they dangled over the water next to hers. "He was there Amelia, he was there all the time." The female turned and looked up at him, shaking her head in frustration. "Amelia," he continued, pleading to her better judgement. "Amelia, he must have been at the brook. Maybe even watching us. How could he have been at the same place at the same time if he wasn't following us?" he finished, returning his gaze across the water.

Lifting her feet back onto the platform, Amelia furiously threw the flower she had been playing with into the water beneath them. "Pongo, that's so mean," she snapped at him. "Sabah got lost, just like we did!" she shouted, as she stood up and started moving away. "Just because you don't like him, you always want to think bad of him!" she yelled at her stunned friend.

Stopping in her tracks, the angry female turned back to her mate, raising her finger to point at him. "Besides you have to remember, it was YOU who took us from the group, YOU who got us lost, YOU who left me with the creature!" she shouted, turning on her heels and striding furiously into the nearest building.

Pongo sat in silence, shattered at what he'd just heard, his head hanging low with feelings of both sadness and guilt coursing through his veins.

Sitting with his legs still dangling over the edge, plucking randomly at the red fur that covered them; the young ape wondered where all of this would end up. *Would Amelia become his rival's sweetheart after all? Would he ever see his home again?* Twirling the red fur through his long waxy fingers, he watched as the flower Amelia had just thrown drifted across the water. Dismayed, he longed to go back just a few days to the carefree sunny afternoon at the brook, to the safety of the group, to his mother and moreover, back into Amelia's heart.

The remainder of the evening was spent sitting on the various nests that Amelia called a bed and eating the haul of fruit and plants Sabah had returned with.

Pongo was quiet. His heart was bruised as well as his ego and now he sat watching on at Amelia laughing endlessly at Sabah's stories. No matter how hard it was to hear this from his sweetheart, there was much truth in what she had said and the young ape spent the last few hours reflecting on her words, each one bruising his already forlorn heart.

Despite this, a plan was formed that night where the three apes would embark on a short trip the next day; to see if Amelia could remember any walks she had taken as a child. It was also decided that they would use some of the human tools to create markings, which could guide them both to and from the shelter. But for now, they lay down on these funny human beds to sleep for the night, to rest before their next adventure would begin.

It was a strange experience for Pongo, lying in this building, where there was no sound, no stars, no breeze or moon to look at. He had never gone to sleep without being able to see the night sky, and he found himself struggling to fall asleep this night. Eventually, after being restless for some time, he moved to a bed near an opening Amelia had called a window, where he could finally see the moon and a few twinkling stars. As he looked up at its big round white face, he hoped his mother was looking at it too, wondering to himself if she could see the same small cloud that was gliding in front of it and the star that was twinkling alongside. The young male started to trace his mother's image over and over in his mind; bringing him some much needed comfort and helping ease his troubled mind to sleep.

Little boy lost

Henry anxiously looked around him, tears beginning to well up in his eyes as the realisation sank in that he was completely lost. The bush that was in front of him was as dense as that behind and all traces of where he'd just crawled from had by now disappeared as the plants naturally popped back to their original position, quickly eliminating signs of disturbance.

Slowly moving forward, the small boy pushed through bushes and branches hoping to find a clearing. However, the dense foliage was unrelenting and scratched at his skin while other plants seemed to extend spiky twigs from all directions that caught on his clothes as he passed by, slowing his journey considerably.

By now, the sun was beginning to fall from the sky and the young boy began to shiver from both fear and the cool evening air; his shorts and thin white shirt proving no match for this harsh jungle environment.

Henry started crying to himself, sobbing softly under his breath while continuing to call out for his Mum and Dad.

The noise of the jungle began to change as the buzz of the daily creatures faded away, leaving only the cries of nocturnal animals echoing through the still of the night.

His surroundings were now bathed in a dark green dusky hue, causing eerie shadows to appear that scared the young boy. His imagination conjured up ideas that they were wild animals looking for their evening meal. Moving quickly, he began looking for anything that would provide warmth, shelter and safety away from these frightening surroundings.

Finally breaking through the bush, Henry found a clearing and began looking around for somewhere to hide, his tiny frame almost lost amongst the giant woody structures that soared above him.

The boy moved toward several of the trees, circling their trunks looking for a hollow that he could fit in. He used his hands to glide over the stumps, feeling for nooks not visible to the eye. Before long, he found one. A few feet from the ground, there was a cavity. He looked up at it, wondering what was inside and decided to climb up and look.

Reaching up, Henry grasped a knobby bump on the side of the trunk and hauled himself off the ground, following through with his leg as he lifted it onto another notch and secured his position. From here the young boy was able to reach the lip of the hollow and pull himself in, heaving his body up and over the bumpy edge and into a space within the belly of the tree.

For a moment the exhausted boy just lay there, breathing heavily and looking around him, trying to absorb his surroundings in this quickly fading light.

Using his hands, he felt beneath him where over time sticks, leaves and brush had gathered, creating a warm nest for him to sleep on. This, he decided right away, would be his bed for the night.

The small boy turned on his side, humming a lullaby under his breath that his mother would sing to him, in an attempt to drown out the sounds outside of the tree. As he began to drift off, he was certain that tomorrow his father would find him and he would go home, and that he would soon be in his own bed with his mother beside him and his sister in her cot. Henry let out a big sigh and fell asleep, he was hungry and exhausted but for now he was safe.

Henry woke to the feeling of something pecking intermittently at his leg. Opening his eyes in response, he came face to face with a brown speckled owl sitting at the opening of the hollow, her huge yellow eyes and piercing black pupils staring directly at him while her sharp pointed beak continued pecking down toward his leg.

The startled boy jumped backwards further into the cavity having never seen a bird so big, while the owl stayed put, turning its head this way and that to look at him, trying to work out if he was a threat or not.

With the light now streaming in through the opening, the small boy spotted a lone speckled egg where he was just laying and could now see that where he slept was in fact a neatly made nest; most likely this bird's nest and more than likely her egg.

Taking a step into the hollow, the owl moved towards him, her talon like claws reaching toward the egg; gently tapping it and turning it over to check it was ok, before puffing up her feathers and circling, finally settling herself on top of the object.

Henry stayed frozen in place, pinned against the back of this woody cave, wondering just how he was going to escape it. But after a few moments he noticed the owl tuck her head under her wing and start to sleep, tired after a night of foraging and hunting throughout the jungle.

Slowly the boy started to slide his body around the edge of the nook, trying not to wake or disturb the sleeping bird as he quietly made his way toward the opening. Slipping one leg out at a time, the small child looked back as he prepared to release his grip.

At the same time, the bird lifted her head from her wing, casting him one final hypnotic glance before returning to her sleep and allowing the young boy to be on his way.

Henry's feet hit the floor with a thud as he made his descent from the tree. Immediately observing the area, the boy was surprised how different everything looked in the daylight and he spent a moment surveying the location, taking in the beauty that he'd not been able to see the night before. Gone were the eerie shadows that seemed to appear from nowhere, leaving in its place a picturesque scene of trees and lush plants with butterflies darting in between.

Instantly feeling hopeful, the young boy made a plan, he would start walking and see if he could find someone that might help him and maybe if he was lucky he would find something to eat. He was so hungry his stomach was beginning to grumble so loudly that it sounded like some of the creatures from the previous night.

With a spring in his step, Henry quickly moved through the woods, the sunlight warming his cool body while the rays of light directed him to clearer paths and away from the denser bush land.

The smell of smoke was still lingering in the air, but the small boy paid no attention to it. For all he knew, forests always smelled of smoke. His concern was to find food and getting home.

Soon after, the young boy came across some fruit trees randomly situated in the middle of the jungle. Looking around nervously, he reached for a branch and plucked off what appeared to be a pear and sat down on the ground to eat it. With juice still tumbling down his chin, Henry ran to the next plant and pulled at some bright pink fruits covered in spiky skin, devouring them as quickly as possible.

Running from one fruit tree to another, the young boy stayed in the garden for as long as he could, consuming as much as he was able until his belly was so full it ached, and his eyes had become weary from eating too much.

Looking around, Henry wondered, *Why such a garden would be here. In the middle of the jungle, whose could it be?* With his tummy still sore, he decided to explore the area to see if anyone was here and set off to look around the place. It wasn't long before the small boy found some abandoned buildings. The huts were all built from wood and were adjacent to some water. Hoping someone was here, he cried out, stopping and listening for any reply but there was nothing. Again he yelled out, but still no one answered.

Cautiously, he entered the buildings and realised instantly that no one lived there as furniture lay broken and strewn across the place while many birds had made their nests on the floors and up in the eaves of the roof.

Slowly as he walked around the empty rooms he wondered whom this place belonged to and where they might have gone. Continuing to explore the place, he walked toward the next building, which immediately reminded him of the dormitory rooms at his school. In these rooms were endless small beds, one after the other, side by side along both sides of the room. The boy frowned. *Why would so many children live out here, in the middle of the jungle?* He wondered to himself, as he looked up and down the length of the room.

Puzzled, he sat on a bed taking in the surroundings, unsure as to what this place was. Reaching for the last piece of fruit in his pocket, the young boy laid back and stared at the ceiling, eating what remained of the langsat fruit and reflecting on his day so far.

The rays of the afternoon sun now moved beyond the window and a gentle breeze blew in, offering a welcomed relief from the humidity.

At the same time, the last blast of sugary energy from the recently devoured fruit subsided, leaving Henry feeling lethargic and ready for a siesta. Soon his almond shaped eyes began to close, succumbing to the comfort of the rickety old bed and the fullness in his tummy.

The three young apes spent the day surveying the local area, looking for any signs that Amelia might remember. It had been a few years since she was here and the landscape had changed considerably with fresh new growth taking place of tired fallen trees, making it difficult for the young female to be certain of which way was which.

Pongo's job was to mark the stumps and trunks along the way in order to provide guidance back to the buildings and to prevent them following the same path on future trips, while Sabah and his now devoted companion Amelia, scouted the treetops for anything of recognition.

The day's search was fruitless. The time that had passed between then and now had altered the landscape so much that there was nothing of significance that Amelia could detect. Feeling deflated after what was an uneventful day, the three apes headed back to the shelter to eat and sleep for the night and prepare for another trip tomorrow.

By now, the bond growing between his two companions was becoming obvious as their displays of affection grew and Pongo found himself wondering how long he should stay with the two of them. *Maybe there was no chance of Amelia remembering where she had been taken years before, leaving the three of them lost in the jungle forever. In which case, when should he separate from them and make his own way in the world?*

The young male continued his journey through the vines back to the shelter, his mind mulling over the various options, frustrated at the lack of progress, while at the same time wondering what tomorrow would bring. There was a faint smell of smoke in the air, which wasn't unusual but it was something that he thought he should take notice of. Flaring his nostrils in response, the young male inhaled, taking note of how strong the smell was for future reference and in which direction it was likely to be coming from.

As they neared the buildings Sabah offered to go and collect fruit for them all again, leaving the former friends alone, awkwardly traversing the remaining trees which would lead them back to the shelter. Arriving at their destination, Amelia wasted no time in moving away from her mate, leaving him to sit on the platform alone once more, watching as small birds skipped across the top of the water, gathering insects for an afternoon feed.

"Pongo," Amelia's voice whispered from behind, breaking through his thoughts. "Pongo, you must come," she repeated, beckoning him with her long limb while looking back inside the room. The young male stood up, throwing the stick he'd just been playing with carelessly into the water, instantly disturbing the feeding birds, causing them to quickly head for the sky.

Moving alongside his friend and taking a look into the room, Pongo could see the silhouette of something laying on one of the beds but he couldn't make out what it was. Cautiously, the ape moved a bit further inside, curiously leaning over the bed and squinting his eyes as they adjusted to the dimmer light. He suddenly realised the shape on the bed was that of a small human child.

The two apes looked at each other for a moment, not knowing what to say or do. Amelia held no fear toward humans because of her upbringing and used to be able to communicate with them when she was younger, but Pongo had never seen one before and was fascinated to see the likeness between them both. Curiously, he held up his fingers and wriggled them, comparing them to that of the infant's.

Breaking through his thoughts, Amelia began tugging firmly at his arm, gesturing for him to go back outside.

"Sabah will be back any minute," she explained. "He will likely scare the infant so can you keep him away while I try to wake the child and find out where he has come from?"

Leaning back towards the doorway, Pongo stopped to take another look at the sleeping infant and agreed to Amelia's request, wanting nothing more than to please his former sweetheart and hopefully win back some respect.

Regardless of the situation with the child, the young male began to feel something he hadn't in many days; he felt needed, and as he left the buildings to look for his rival, there was an extra spring in his step as he negotiated the woody vines that fell silently from the trees high above.

All hands to deck

Don Henderson stood at the edge of the bush land, a large towel draped over his bare chest, barking orders at the group of men in front of him, yelling over and over to, "just do something!"

Intermittently, he would pace up and down like a wild animal, running his hands through his black hair and muttering to himself about whose fault the situation was.

His son, Henry, had been missing now for several hours with the sun falling quickly from the sky. Don was told by the supervisor that they might have to wait all night before they could look for the child, as it was impossible to track the boy in the dark.

Bayu was performing at his best, having ordered all of the vehicles on site to come to the area and turn their headlights on, flooding the bush land with brilliant light.

Initially the plan was useful as the trackers were able to clearly see the path the young boy had taken and in which direction he had gone. But even with the lights of a dozen trucks illuminating the area like a football field, the beams were not able to penetrate the thick dense edge of the forest that lay ahead, hampering their attempts to track the boy beyond this.

The long dark hours of the night ticked by more slowly than anyone could imagine as the father of the boy and his crew sat, scattered around the area, hoping and praying the child was safe and well.

Some men positioned themselves high on the bonnets of the trucks, using their binoculars to constantly search for any movement amongst the grasslands that could lead them to him; others sat alone listening intently to the noises of the forest, trying to isolate the different sounds to see if they could pick up the cries of a little boy lost.

After what seemed like an eternity, the first rays of light peeked through the trees, bringing with it warmth that instantly took the chill off the cool night air. Simultaneously the noise of the forest began to escalate, producing a high-pitched melody as one by one, its inhabitants came to life.

Immediately, the work site became a flurry of activity as the men began to assemble themselves and their kits, ready to start tracking the young boy.

Bayu was first to be ready, having not slept at all the previous night. Quickly he moved amongst the workmen, picking who would travel with him to start searching the denser woodlands, tapping them on the shoulders and issuing instructions as to where they would meet up.

Not present was Don, who had retired to the cabin during the early hours of the morning, having become overwhelmed with emotion.

By right, the supervisor should be waking his boss to get ready to leave, but Bayu knew Don had no tracking skills and in his current emotional state, he could easily jeopardise the search. Besides, if they were to find the young boy injured or worse, having a distraught parent with them would not benefit the situation at all.

Instead, the supervisor decided that his own father, Wayan, plus a few of the other men, would wake Don in a few more hours, and bring him with them at that time; giving himself and his trackers a good head start and hopefully a happy resolution.

With the area now bathed in a warm orange glow, the men set off to the edge of the forest and the last place they'd been able to place the boy. Carefully the men studied the low-lying foliage, looking for signs of disruption, from broken blades of grass to soil that showed signs of recent movement. Slowly, bit by bit, they were able to identify Henry's movements and the direction in which he appeared to have travelled.

However, nothing on this journey was easy, with the group having to move through dense bush land, sometimes losing the trail amongst the thicker sections that proved more difficult to negotiate.

Bewildered, Bayu wondered how on earth the small boy had gotten this far, at some points even doubting their own tracking ability.

If it wasn't for the steady stream of clues they discovered, he would not have believed it possible that someone so small was capable of such an arduous trek.

Many hours passed by before the men were out of the dense scrub and standing freely in a clearing, eagerly drinking from their water bottles while dusting debris from their worn and tired bodies.

Surveying the surrounding area for more clues, the trackers noticed a tree that had recently been disturbed, spotting some sticks and leaves that lay scattered on the ground beneath its solid round trunk.

Their eyes quickly moved up the body of the tree where they could see a hollow about halfway up from where the pieces on the ground had fallen. With lightening reaction, Bayu and his men raced toward it, calling out the boy's name in the hope he was inside. It wasn't to be, for at that moment a large tawny owl looked out from her nest, widening and dilating her eyes at the sight of the men in front of her.

The men slumped down to the ground in frustration, opening their water bottles once more while continuing to look around the area for more clues.

Taking this as an opportunity for a rest, the supervisor sat in the clearing drinking from his own canister, trying to work out the boy's next moves from here. As he looked around, Bayu picked up on the increasing smell of smoke and glanced up to see birds circling areas that were likely being destroyed by the fire that was still burning deep within the woods.

Increasingly aware that time was against them, the supervisor stood and summoned his men to finish what they were doing and keep moving. The sun was now slipping from the sky, meaning daylight was running out for both themselves as well as for the young child who would then be faced with a second night in the jungle.

An uninvited guest

Amelia sat quietly on the platform outside the buildings waiting for the sleeping child to stir. Shards of red light reflected from her orange fur as the afternoon rays of the sun danced across her body on its journey back towards the earth.

The young female had not had a moment to truly reflect on the past few days, or how surreal it was to be sitting here again, alone amongst the empty buildings. But as she sat there reminiscing, the quiet that had encompassed the vacant shelter for so long slowly began to come to life in her mind. Soon, the place she had called home was alive once more with the shrieks of infant orangutan's blending effortlessly with the voices of the humans that once cared for them.

Her immediate thoughts turned to Joy, and she smiled, remembering the older lady with greying hair tied up into a loose bun on top of her head.

Joy had taken care of the infants or wounded apes as they arrived at the shelter. Sometimes they would be injured or burned while other times they were so young, so very little, that it was a struggle for them to survive.

The carer was a stern lady with a funny voice, Amelia thought someone once said she was from a place known as Scots land. But regardless of opinion, the young female always knew that Joy had a soft heart. Because sometimes at night, once the infants were all in bed, Amelia would hear her crying and crying, usually after a number of new apes had been found and especially when some hadn't survived, be it mother or infant.

Then there was Dan, a practical man who looked after the apes outside of the shelter. He was the man that had led her to Ma's tree and he had been the last human she had seen.

He didn't live here like Joy. Rather, he came and went quite often, but when he was at the shelter he usually sat and worked at a place called a desk, busy with books and papers.

Dan was nice but he didn't cuddle or feed the infants like Joy or the other ladies; instead he would look into their ears, or shine things in their eyes, and if anyone was sick, it was Dan who tried to fix them.

Sitting in the afternoon sun, Amelia surveyed the area, casting her mind back to moments of fun with all of her young friends. She looked at the vines that they would swing from, and could still hear the shrieks of laughter as they fell with a thud into the water beneath. Turning her gaze towards the trees she could still see the dozens of red infantile bodies scrambling through the branches, chasing each other around, with an abundance of laughter as they tried desperately to out manoeuvre each other.

Softly smiling to herself, the young ape never realised how much this place meant to her. While the jungle was now her home; sitting here, alone in the afternoon sun, Amelia realised what a special place this had been and how fond of it she was.

Looking around, a touch of sadness coming over her, the young female questioned where everyone had gone and why? There were so many new babies when she left, *Surely they couldn't all have been taken to the jungle?* She wondered to herself.

Shaking her head, Amelia stood and began to move toward the room where the young boy was sleeping, anticipating just how she would wake him, without scaring the small child to bits. But as she turned, her eyes locked with the eyes of the orange striped beast! He stood directly in front of her, his body lowered, one paw forward, ready to pounce.

A moment passed that felt like eternity as Amelia, unable to move, held the gaze of the creature. His yellow green eyes penetrated her body to the core as his muscles rippled and his yellow stained fangs glistened with saliva, ready to devour his next meal.

Moving as quickly as she could, Amelia leapt through the doorway to where the child slept, heavy thuds now thundering behind her.

Grabbing at the sleeping child, she lifted him up without a thought, taking hold of a beam positioned close by on the ceiling and propelled them both forward.

Henry was screaming at the top of his lungs as the tiger appeared behind them, barging into the room and leaping across the bed that he had just been sleeping on, turning it completely on its side. Amelia jumped higher still, dragging the small boy along as the beast closed in on them, roaring at the top of its lungs, scaring Henry to the core.

The boy continued screaming, unsure of who was out to harm him, if not both of these creatures. Amelia just kept moving, using her knowledge of the immediate area to lift the pair high up into the trees and away from the jaws of this giant beast.

At last, they found a perch that was high above the buildings where they were able to sit and watch as the tiger sauntered back and forth looking up towards them, grumbling and growling under his breath.

The small boy was now sobbing heavily, his tiny body shaking with fear as he wondered if this red ape had indeed saved him, or just saved him for dinner?

Immediately sensing this, the gentle female drew upon her human skills and began to pacify the young boy, at first by rubbing his head and arms, and then soothing him by wiping away his tears.

Using her long arm, she reached out of the perch and pulled at a leaf, gently cupping it before passing it to him, allowing him to drink its contents of fresh rainwater; but more importantly, doing something to gain his trust.

It worked; Henry stopped crying and raised his arm to wipe away the tears from his face while glancing about at his immediate surroundings. Looking down toward the buildings, the boy gasped at just how high they were and for a moment he seemed a little unsteady, but gently his red companion raised her finger and placed it under his chin, softly lifting it up and shaking her head for him not to look.

For some time, the unusual pair huddled together high up in the tree providing each other comfort and security. The tiger had laid his bulky body down beneath them, spread out on the platform where Amelia had just been sitting, fully prepared to wait it out this time for his next meal.

Henry carefully shifted himself closer to the female ape for warmth as the sun disappeared, resting his head on her chest, nestling amongst the thickness of her coarse red fur.

Beneath them the throaty purr of the tiger continued to permeate through the trees, a constant reminder of his presence below them along with the crackling sound of a nearby fire.

Amelia's thoughts turned to her two friends who should have been back already and fearfully she wondered if the beast had come across them first.

Quickly dismissing that thought from her mind, the female ape instinctively put her arm around the young boy's shoulders, attempting to protect him from the cool night air that was now whistling through the treetops.

Puffing up her coat against the chilly breeze, the pair settled in for what would be a very long night. Amelia knew she would have to try and stay awake in order to keep the boy safe and prevent him from toppling out of the tree as well as look out for her friends. Tomorrow, if they had not returned, she would have to find a way to save both the youngster and herself and escape the striped creature that was sleeping beneath them.

Friend or Foe?

Not long after leaving Amelia at the shelter, Pongo arrived at the orchard to find Sabah sitting on the floor under a large tree, devouring copious amounts of fresh food as fast as he was able.

Looking up, the greedy ape noticed his friend approaching and with a lightening sharp reaction, dropped the remaining pieces and stood up, shuffling together some fruits with his feet that lay scattered on the floor around him.

Surveying the ground where the older ape was just sitting, Pongo noticed remnants of half eaten produce all over the place, from stones to pips and cores, carelessly discarded where Sabah had thrown them during his solo feast. The younger male should not have been surprised, in fact he should have expected this, but as he looked around the area, he quietly shook his head and wondered how Amelia could possibly be falling for this selfish ape's charms.

Bending down and collecting items from the floor, Pongo began to tell his rival about the discovery of the small child, explaining that Amelia thought she was best to be alone with the child when he woke.

Sabah listened on, pretending not to show any interest in what the young male was telling him. He had formed a bond with Amelia now and would demonstrate more enthusiasm when the story came from her.

The two males had not been alone since Sabah revealed he had seen the tiger that attacked Amelia, and the younger male decided there was nothing to lose by questioning him as to why he was there.

"Sabah, you know when you saw the creature you called a tiger?" he began quizzing his rival. "How did you see that? How were you there at the exact same place as Amelia and I, at the same time?" He stopped what he was doing and stood upright to look the other ape in the eye, anticipating another garbled excuse.

"Because I'd been watching you," the older ape confessed without hesitation, a smirk spreading across his face.

Continuing with what he was doing, the devious ape shrugged his shoulders and sneered. "You're so stupid Pongo, I was always going to get her, and now," he paused looking up at the younger ape, "she wouldn't believe you even if you told her!" he said puffing out his chest and laughing.

Furiously Pongo looked away. *He had been right after all,* he thought to himself. Sabah was there the day they were at the brook, he had been spying on them, but his rival was also correct in saying Amelia would never believe him, she didn't believe anything Pongo said now. Filled with rage, the young ape bent down to collect the last of his haul and prepared to start his journey back to the shelter before darkness ensued.

Look over there

Bayu stood in the clearing, unsure of which way to go next. Apart from the debris that had fallen from the hollow in the tree, there was little else to say which way the boy had gone. The men looked around, trying to find that one significant clue that would point them in the right direction. But the area was large and Henry could have taken one of several options, leaving the men with no choice but to continue their journey the best way they could.

Time was now working against them as the sun was starting to fall quickly from the sky, the rays turning from a bright golden light to a warm orange glow as it made its way back towards the earth. Bayu glanced upwards at the setting sun and then back down to his watch, deciding to give the team just one more hour before making a camp for the night and resuming their search the following morning.

Continuing their journey through the trees, the group of men scrutinised everything for any recent movement other than that of the local wildlife that was scurrying around them.

Occasionally there would be a noise in the forest, which would stop the men in their tracks. Bayu would quickly raise his hand and signal for the team to cease movement and draw their weapons, ready to shoot anything that may try and attack them. Mostly, however, they had only encountered small rodents and a few wild pigs that appeared to be on a mission that did not concern them, possibly out running the fire that was burning somewhere deeper within the forest.

By now the sun was beginning to set and Bayu's focus had shifted from looking for the boy to finding a safe area for the night where the search team could rest.

Scouring the immediate area, the young man became aware of some trees that looked as if they bore fruit. Immediately he signalled for the men to follow him as he walked further into the enclosure, plucking something from a nearby plant and biting into its soft fleshy skin.

Wiping at the juice that was running over his chin, the supervisor was happy that this would make a good place to camp for the night and proceeded to unladen himself of his weapon and backpack, grabbing at some more fruit as he moved around the new location, wondering if Henry had found this place also.

Suddenly, without warning, there was movement in the bushes in front of him. Dropping the fruit he had been eating, Bayu darted back to where his gun was, gesturing toward the men to do the same and commanding them to take aim. The men lowered their bodies in response and squinted their eyes, the fading light preventing them from clearly seeing what was ahead of them while the bushes rustled some more.

Bayu raised his gun and looked through the site, aiming in the direction of the noise. Cocking his rifle and slowing his breathing, the young man focused on the bushes ahead. *Threat or not,* he thought to himself, *whatever was in the bush could be dinner for the night.*

Pongo was unaware that they had been noticed as he prepared to leave the orchard and make his way back to the shelter. An unusual sound alerted him, causing him to look up from what he was doing.

Cautiously peeking through the bushes in front of him, he spotted a human, crouched down low on the ground with his arm outstretched, holding something that was pointing toward them.

Gently reaching toward his companion, Pongo raised his waxy finger and pointed to the men, gesturing that they should leave the area immediately.

Suddenly, out of nowhere came the terrified screams of a child, the piercing cry permeating the air that surrounded them, a prolonged howl that temporarily distracted them all.

Bayu's attention immediately switched to the area the sound was coming from, his gun falling slack as he momentarily lost concentration on the target ahead.

Pongo was quick to make the most of the opportunity, grabbing his friend's muscular arm to escape the isolated fruit trees, they swiftly moved out of sight of the humans in front of them.

Bayu immediately noticed the pair scurrying away and signalled to his men to stand down, allowing the apes to go free. *This night had been a lucky one for them,* the young man thought to himself.

With darkness now descending upon them, there was little more the men could do to locate the origin of the screams, knowing that sound could travel in any direction through the forest.

Trying to find the child tonight would be an almost impossible task, the frustrated supervisor thought.

While it was not ideal, he knew they had to call off the search for the night and hope that the boy was still alive and well tomorrow.

The two male apes sat high up in a tree, knowing their movement could attract unwanted attention, putting both of their lives at risk.

The humans were sitting directly beneath them, talking in their funny language while eating the fruit from the surrounding trees and warming themselves next to a small open fire. Watching them, Pongo presumed these humans must be looking for the young boy, but his fear now was that they might consider Amelia a threat.

Both apes also heard the child scream and wondered what had scared him. *Hopefully,* they thought, *it was just the shock of waking to their friend.*

Sitting high in the tree, exposed, cold and lonely, the two males moved closer to each other for warmth, settling in for a night that would be long for both of them. Surprisingly, as they whiled away the hours, the pair began swapping stories and funny anecdotes, not realising how much they had in common; at some points even enjoying each other's company as they waited for the sun to rise.

No one noticed the increasing smell of smoke as the small fire that was burning in the camp disguised it with its own woody scented plumes. Neither did they hear the crackling and popping of the blaze edging closer to them, lost amongst the banter and chatter of the men sitting beneath the pair of apes.

The only warning of the fire that was visible was an orange red glow, deep within the belly of the forest, still very much alive as it burned its way towards them.

Soon the camp was quiet as the men, along with the two apes began to sleep off what had been a tiring day for all concerned.

We're here for
the same thing

Bayu opened his eyes to complete darkness, the strong smell of smoke now filling his nostrils, instantly waking him from his deep sleep. Jumping to his feet the young supervisor moved quickly amongst his men, rousing them one by one and instructing them to pack their stuff together immediately.

The wind was now blowing toward them, carrying the smell of burning wood directly through the site while the crackling and popping of a nearby fire was distinctly audible as it moved quickly in their direction.

Beginning to climb a nearby tree, Bayu scaled its rugged trunk, hoisting himself up with ease so he could properly survey the surrounding landscape, looking for signs of the blaze.

Yelling down to his men, the supervisor revealed that the fire was burning further down the gully and while it was still dark, the men should start moving away from it now.

Chaos was beginning to unfold beneath the apes, and as Pongo looked down he noticed the man he had seen the previous day climbing a nearby tree, using both his hands and feet, as he would himself, to quickly ascend the trunk.

Sensing he was being watched, Bayu glanced through the branches and spotted two apes perched in a tree, their red furry bodies standing out against the dark waxy leaves. Raising his arm, the supervisor tried to shoo the pair away. "Go on, get out of here!" he mouthed at them, pointing toward the fires and waving his arm at them again, but the pair remained where they were.

Taking an interest in the supervisor, the younger ape began observing the movements of his human counterpart, tilting his head as he compared them to his own. He watched curiously as the man raised his finger and pointed it, the younger ape following his lead by holding up his own long wrinkled finger;

then waving his arm back at the man in a magnificent attempt to shoo the young man away.

Bayu stopped what he was doing and laughed. *Had the ape really just copied what he had done or were his eyes playing tricks on him?* He thought to himself, slightly taken aback by the interaction.

Aware that the clock was ticking, the supervisor knew he could not waste precious minutes trying to communicate with a wild animal, especially with the fire burning so close by and threatening them all.

Nodding his head in the direction of the apes, Bayu started making his way back down the trunk of the tree, flicking his hand at the pair as he continued his descent in a final attempt to get them to move.

Stopping suddenly, he turned back and looked toward the smarter of the two apes. "I don't suppose you've seen a child?" he jokingly yelled, using his free hand to describe a small child as best as he was able.

The young supervisor could not be more astonished as Pongo raised his fur covered arm and pointed in the direction of the fires, while moving his hands in what could easily be interpreted as a reference to the young boy.

Shaking his head and laughing in disbelief, the young man continued his journey back to the ground, once again nodding toward the ape and signalling for them to get away.

Jumping the last few feet from the trunk, the supervisor landed with a small thud to the ground, dusting himself off as he looked back up to where the apes had been sitting. To his relief he noticed the pair were no longer there. The tree they had been perched in was now empty.

Bayu continued rounding up his men and prepared for the team to leave; the half-light making it easier to negotiate their way through the wild jungle terrain and away from danger.

However, the encounter with the ape was still playing on his mind, and the young man found himself wondering if the ape had indeed seen the boy. Taking a moment to glance back to the empty tree and then over to the area just ahead of the fires, the supervisor decided he would not be able to live with himself if he didn't check it out.

Signalling to his men the change of direction, Bayu quickly picked up pace as they headed towards the gully and hopefully the place where they would find Henry.

Throughout the journey, Bayu would occasionally catch sight of the two apes traveling ahead of them, traversing the trees and appearing to stay close to the group as they followed the same route.

It was true, the two apes were deliberately moving slower than they were both capable of as they proceeded through the forest, just a few trees in front of the humans. Sabah was unsure as to why they would be leading these men back to the shelter, he thought the idea both risky and stupid. But Pongo had a plan; the quick-thinking youngster thought that if he helped the man find the child, then Amelia would not be harmed when they located them.

With their differing opinions, the two male apes continued steadily through the trees toward the shelter, occasionally rustling some leaves or swinging on a vine, doing just enough for the humans to keep sight of them and hopefully follow their lead.

Eventually, the party came across the abandoned buildings, which were now bathed in a green misty light. A mass of low lying smog that had settled in the gully was preventing the rays of the morning sun from penetrating it, casting an eerie ghostly feel across the area.

Immediately, Pongo set about searching the area for Amelia, using his vantage point to scour the deserted buildings below them.

While down on the ground, the search party stood at the water's edge, squinting their eyes against the smoke and covering their mouths from its fumes, straining to see just a few feet ahead.

A sharp gust of wind blew into the area, instantly causing the smoke to disperse and allowing for a moment of clear vision.

Immediately the supervisor jumped back, gasping at the sight that met his eyes, while his men reached for their weapons and hurriedly raised them to their shoulders.

Looking down, both apes also recoiled with fear as through the mist, the familiar gold and black stripes of a tiger revealed itself, its muscular body spread out majestically on the platform and piercing green eyes gazing right back across the water toward them.

The Rescue

The young supervisor gave the signal to his team to stay quiet but keep their weapons drawn as the wall of smoke slowly returned between the group of men and the tiger, once again reducing their visibility.

Nervously, the apes sat together, continually scouring the area for any sight of Amelia and the child, beginning to fear the worst when they could see no sign of life beyond that of the tiger.

Looking down, Pongo noticed the young supervisor beginning to scale the trunk of a nearby tree. The man headed in the direction of the apes, who watched as he edged closer to them. Having little trust for the humans, Sabah nervously nudged his friend, suggesting they should leave immediately, but Pongo felt the man was not here to harm them and gestured for his companion to relax.

Scrambling through the branches, Bayu wanted to reach the same vantage point as the apes, giving him a bird's eye view of the tiger and an opportunity to shoot the dangerous creature.

Pongo continued to watch as the man came up alongside them and immediately reached for the weapon on his back. For a few moments, nothing happened as he sat motionless alongside the two apes, waiting for the perfect shot.

Without warning, an almighty boom came from beside them, the noise reverberating through the woodlands causing birds to screech and take flight while small animals quickly scurried to safer locations.

Jumping back with fear, the two apes haphazardly grasped hold of some nearby vines, trying to steady themselves, the shock of the blast causing them to temporarily lose balance.

While across the water, the majestic beast let out a piercing shriek as the bullet connected with his flesh, prompting a second wave of birds to head for the skies as the tiger continued to wail in pain.

At the same time the sound of a child crying echoed through the forest, the high pitched wail distracting

Bayu once again, prompting him to lower his weapon as he vigorously scrutinised the surrounding trees for the boy.

The two apes lifted themselves back up and immediately started to search the nearby forest. Pongo strained to reach a higher branch, stretching his flexible body to examine every square inch of the area.

Suddenly a huge wave of relief washed over him as the familiar shape of his friend caught his eye. Looking across the expanse, the young ape could see not one, but two bodies perched high up across the water from them, safely out of reach of the tiger.

Beating his chest, and raising his arms, Pongo did his best to attract the attention of the supervisor, trying to alert him to the location of both Amelia and the child.

However no matter how animated his gestures were they appeared to be going unnoticed by the man. Frustrated, Pongo turned to his companion for some help, suggesting that they both put on a display for him.

Sabah was still unsure as to why they would want to help the humans. *It was after all, them that were causing these fires*, he thought to himself.

The older ape didn't care if the humans lost a child in the forest, he had lost many friends himself, as giant infernos chased them from their homes and in many cases took their lives as well.

Pongo lived in a dream world, he scoffed as he watched the young ape perform. *A fairy-tale world of brook meetings, butterflies and birds,* he thought, quietly shaking his head at his companion's naivety.

Unfortunately, life wasn't like the young ape thought and Sabah had seen it firsthand. With his own eyes, he had witnessed what these humans did when they came to the forest and ripped out the trees, burning their stumps to the ground before planting row after row of new palm trees, leaving nowhere for the native wildlife to live.

Sabah knew Pongo was too young to have visited these sites to see the destruction for himself, but unbeknown to the young ape, Sabah HAD been there, secretly travelling with a group of much older males who were intent on finding out the truth about the fires.

Sabah could never forget the day when as far has his eyes could see, the jungle had disappeared, never to be replaced as it was burned from existence to make way for their new palm trees. Men, like the one in the tree alongside him, came every day and took more and more forest, while caring nothing for wounded wildlife, instead leaving them to fend for themselves or to die where they lay. It was at that moment Sabah knew nowhere was safe, not even the branch he was perched on now, and the jungle would be lost forever to the greedy humans and their palm trees.

"I see him, I see him." A voice broke through Sabah's thoughts, prompting him to look across at the human, watching as he shouted down to the others while pointing in the direction of Henry and Amelia.

Raising his arm, Bayu waved toward the young child. "Henry!" he shouted across the expanse. "Henry, we are here to help you, are you ok?" he bellowed, relieved to see the young boy alive and well, while cautiously observing the ape alongside him.

The boy lifted his arm to acknowledge the supervisor, seemingly unfazed by the creature he was trapped with, as he reassured the man he was ok.

Bayu watched as the ape alongside the boy appeared to be communicating back and forth to the two that were perched beside him; using a series of high pitch sounds and dramatic gestures. Observing the display, the supervisor sensed that the group must be known to each other. *Which was lucky,* he thought to himself, for if he believed the ape with Henry was a solitary animal, he would have considered it a threat and most likely taken his best shot at it.

Shifting his gaze beyond them all, the supervisor looked to the area where the fire appeared to be coming from. Raising his binoculars, he began to slowly survey the jungle as he tried to work out the safest and quickest way to reach the tree where the small boy was trapped.

It would be far too risky to send his men across the smog covered water, directly toward the shelter and the injured tiger. But looking beyond the child, he could see flames rapidly approaching, cutting them off from the rear. Bayu let the binoculars go, the bulky item coming to rest with a thud against his chest, as he rubbed his eyes with his hands; the mixture of wind and smoke now blurring his vision. Bayu sighed, he had to find a solution and he had to find it fast.

The noise of the forest could not disguise the throaty growls of Wulan the Great as he limped from room to room inside the empty buildings. Occasionally he flopped to the floor to lick his weeping wound; keeping his pale green eyes fixed firmly on any openings.

Wulan was a five year old Sumatran tiger with golden fur and strong black stripes that ran vertically down his body, providing camouflage in his native jungle.

The majestic animal had encountered humans before on his travels, learning that no matter what his own strength, power or size that these men were able to bring down his species in an instant.

Life had become difficult in the forest since the people and their machines arrived. The tracks he would follow as a young cub had all but gone, replaced by lines of plants that native animals were not able to live amongst as they offered neither food nor protection.

Eventually the changes to the forest had forced creatures like Wulan to move deeper and deeper into the jungle, competing with each other to find food and survive in a much smaller area.

Laying in the shelter, tending his open wound, the tiger reflected on how many times recently he had gone without meals. His stomach had become hollow and his hips now protruded through his once muscular frame as he endured the harsher environment the situation was causing.

However, there were many that weren't as lucky as him, some had succumbed to starvation while others lost their lives by the hand of these men as they desperately hunted for food amongst the new trees, hunger taking the place of caution.

And now, here he was, stuck in this cabin wounded, hungry and afraid, wondering if this might be the day that one more Sumatran tiger disappeared from the jungle, before the jungle disappeared itself.

Pongo used his vantage point to reach the same conclusion as the human. He could see the fire at the rear, and while he couldn't see the striped beast in the buildings, he could hear the animal's groans from within. The tiger was alive.

Moving quickly through the treetops, the young ape curled his toes around a branch, and allowed his body to drop into an empty space, twirling around freely, checking as many angles as possible.

With only some low smog now obstructing his view, Pongo searched the buildings from top to bottom, the familiar stripes of the beast soon catching his eye. At the rear of one of the bedrooms he observed the tiger lying slumped on the floor, seemingly tending to an open wound.

The size of the beast WAS a little daunting, but the young ape knew that if the animal was injured, it would slow his reactions down considerably. Immediately the youngster began to hatch a plan while motioning for his friend to join him, hastily relaying his thoughts to his companion.

Sabah listened intently, his eyes surveying the area as his friend talked, deciding for himself if the plan would work. He knew the humans would take to their weapons given the chance. But what choice was there? He could now hear the fire approaching, its fierce roar growing louder as it sped towards them, tearing down all that stood in its path.

Agreeing to the plan, Sabah prepared to move through the branches toward Amelia. Meanwhile

Pongo surveyed the empty buildings, planning how he would use his knowledge of the layout to distract the tiger and allow his friend to slip past unnoticed.

The pair waited a moment or two for the wall of smoke to rise and provide them some cover before embarking on their journey.

Once on their way, the apes quickly traversed through the vines and arrived at the platform soon after. Sabah checked to see if they had been seen by the humans while the younger ape started to move quietly along the uneven surface, cautiously looking for the wounded animal. Raising his arm, Pongo indicated that he had spotted the beast and signalled for his friend to leave. The trickster acknowledged the gesture with a wave and final cheeky wink.

The pair had never seen eye to eye, but at this moment Pongo was certainly glad of Sabah's help, even feeling for the first time that he could trust the confident male. Watching as his comrade departed the buildings he wondered if after all of this, whether it would be possible to even become good friends.

Returning to the task at hand, the youngster began to move cautiously toward the room where the tiger lay. Nervously he curled his long fingers around the frame of the opening and peeked around the corner to see the beast laying just a few feet away. Immediately the animal acknowledged his arrival with a slow threatening growl.

Not deterred, Pongo looked again, this time revealing himself fully to the tiger, hoping to lure the creature into a pursuit; but the animal just lay there, his lips curled, exposing his stained yellowed fangs, growling but not making any move toward the young ape.

As he was about to make his third attempt, a noise distracted him, causing him to briefly look away. Glancing across the water, he noticed that the crowd was now larger with a number of new men having joined the initial group, one in particular causing quite a commotion.

Deciding it was not a matter to concern him, the ape turned back to the shelter, and returned his gaze to where the tiger had just been laying.

It was now empty, the beast nowhere to be seen. Panicked, the ape began to look around, before feeling an unnerving presence move alongside him.

The breath of the tiger easily engulfed Pongo's small red body, wrapping itself around him like a blanket while the throaty growl made the fur on his neck instantly stand on end. Trembling with fear, the frightened young ape slowly turned around to come face to face with the beast that was standing beside him. Pongo tensed and braced himself for what would come next, closing his eyes as he succumbed to the fate that awaited him.

Bayu was busy instructing his team as to their next move when he became aware of a disturbance somewhere in the bushes behind them. Raising his arm in response, the supervisor quickly signalled to the group who immediately crouched down and drew their weapons, preparing themselves for whatever was approaching.

The area came to a complete stand still as the young man tried to identify the source of the commotion; instantly recognising the sound of a familiar voice, and gesturing for his men to lower their weapons.

Bayu was now wearing his shirt tied around his lower face, covering both his mouth and nose to protect him from the increasing fumes. Standing up, the young man loosened it and let it fall around his neck. He coughed immediately as the smoke hit his lungs, while preparing himself to face the wrath of his American boss.

Immediately the supervisor greeted Don Henderson as the group entered the clearing. Wayan, who was travelling alongside him looked tired and drawn, the rough journey having taken its toll on his elderly frame.

The supervisor immediately began to update Don on the whereabouts of Henry, revealing that he was trapped high in a tree.

Offering him his binoculars, the anxious father immediately took them and placed them to his eyes, scouring the woodlands for his son.

The supervisor pointed to the location where the young boy could be seen while explaining that the child was not alone, an ape was trapped there with him. Don lowered the instrument from his eyes and furiously turned to the young man.

"WHY IS THE APE STILL THERE?" he exploded, his cheeks reddening as he reached for the rifle that was slung across his back. "DO I HAVE TO DO EVERYTHING AROUND HERE?" he continued, as he raised the weapon to his flushed face, staring through the scope in the direction of the boy.

As fast as he could, Bayu explained about the tiger and that he believed the ape was of no threat to the child. Hastily he tried to convince the angered father that he had watched them, interacting in a simple manner, and that Henry himself HAD indicated he was ok. The supervisor kept talking, trying to warn his boss that a shot from this distance could in fact harm the child, the expanse was too great, while the rising smoke impaired their vision.

Defiantly, Don held the rifle high, scanning the trees, frantically searching the area for anything that might threaten his son. At that moment, a movement across the expanse caught his eye. The panicked father couldn't be sure if it was anything as the smoke was obscuring his view, but still he held his weapon steady, ready to shoot.

Bayu was now silent, his position with Don had been made clear, it was obvious his words were falling on deaf ears.

As the smoke continued to thicken, the young man tugged at the shirt around his neck, pulling it back up around his face while stepping back, quietly blending in with the men behind him.

It was only mid-afternoon, yet the sky was now black, casting eerie shadows over the shelters and its surroundings. The birds that usually circled overhead were long gone, their panicked screeches now only an echo in the distance as they fled their homes for safer pastures.

All that remained was the noise of the fire, roaring toward them like a steam engine charging through the trees and heading straight in their direction.

The sound of a gunshot cut through the moment, ricocheting through the gully, catching Bayu and his men off guard and causing them to jump in response.

Across the water, an animal shrieked as the bullet crossed the expanse and made contact with it, followed by the sound of a heavy thud as the creature fell to the ground. Don watched through the lens, holding the weapon steady for a second shot should he need it, smoke still unfurling from the warm nozzle.

He didn't, the animal lay motionless where it fell. There was no movement and no sound, as a deathly hush fell over the area.

For a moment it seemed as if the world had stopped, until the wails of the little boy began, his panicked screams growing louder, echoing through the gully and reaching out across the divide.

Amelia and Henry had braved the previous night's cool air. High in the tree, her thick red fur providing warmth and comfort to the small boy in his unfamiliar environment. Sleep had been scarce for the female ape that night as she kept watch, hoping her friends would be nearby and soon be back to help them escape the tree.

During their hours together the small boy came to realise the ape would not harm him, and it appeared she was trying to help him. She had given him water and allowed him to curl into her when he became cold and tired. *She did smell rather badly,* Henry thought, *and her fur was coarse and matted,* but as they sat trapped high in the tree he was able to cast those issues aside, as he knew that she had in fact saved his life.

It was Amelia who first spotted the humans that morning. Sitting high up in the precarious nest she had seen them arrive. She soon noticed her two friends in a nearby tree, relieved to see them both alive and well.

The wafts of smoke that now filled the gully hindered her view of the pair, but through a series of gestures she had managed to make contact, and as sporadic as it was she knew they would come to help her.

Before long, Amelia watched as her two friends quickly moved across the vines and onto the platform of the shelter, before parting company as Sabah continued toward herself and the child.

Smiling, the female ape watched him moving towards them, his long arms propelling him gracefully through the trees as he glided closer to the pair, ready to help rescue them both.

Pulling the young boy closer, the female ape pointed toward her friend as he approached, indicating that he was not a threat and the boy should not be alarmed.

But at that moment a shot rang out, echoing through the trees before leaving an eerie silence in its wake. Amelia shrieked as she watched Sabah begin to fall backwards, tumbling through the branches and breaking them off as he descended quickly towards the ground. Finally, he disappeared out of sight onto the smoky forest floor.

Amelia turned toward the terrified child, instinctively wrapping her long orange limbs around him while holding him tight, trying to soothe his panicked cries. With tears now spilling over her own rounded cheeks, the female buried her head against the boy, her body trembling with fear and shock as the realisation of what just happened took hold. They were trapped and alone. The fire was nearby, their only help was gone, and so too was her friend.

At the same time Pongo was preparing to take the swipe from Wulan's giant paw when the shot rang out, instantly causing the tiger to cower. With his claws still extended, the animal lowered his body in defence, his nails digging in to the wooden planks beneath him as he flattened his large frame in an attempt to reduce his size.

Immediately looking toward the direction of the sound, Wulan turned on his heels and hastily departed the abandoned buildings. His lithe striped body soon disappeared into the woodland beyond them.

Alone on the platform and with his heart still pounding, the young ape began to look around, trying to establish what had just happened.

The smoke was patchy between the young ape and the humans but as it swirled around he caught sight of the man he'd noticed just a few moments ago, with a weapon held up to his face.

Filled with fear, Pongo followed the direction in which it was pointing, quickly realising it was aimed in Amelia's direction.

Panicked, the ape looked across at the tree, searching for any sign of his companions, soon spotting the terrified female embracing the boy. But there was no sign of Sabah and there was no movement in the trees.

With his stomach now beginning to feel queasy, Pongo continued searching the area hoping for one glimpse of the older male's bulky frame; but there was nothing.

With his head beginning to spin, Pongo sank to the floor, his legs trembling before giving way to the weight of his body. "Sabah," the young ape whispered,

tears filling his brown eyes. "NO," he cried to himself.
"Please not Sabah."

Realising there was no time to waste, Pongo immediately picked himself up and wiped the tears from
his face, he had to save Amelia even if he was now
alone. Dusting himself off, he hurried to the far side
of the empty building, ensuring he was out of sight
of the humans across the water. Quickly, the young
ape climbed up the edge of the shack, calling out to
Amelia, and signalling for her to stay put and keep a
tight hold of the boy.

Tearfully the female ape responded, acknowledging his request, shuffling her body closer to the child's
as Pongo had asked.

The sound of the fire was now roaring towards
them and the frightened young male ape knew he had
little time to save the pair, without risking his life along
the way.

Keeping out of sight, Pongo scaled a nearby tree
and began climbing it as fast as he could, knowing

there would be one opportunity to get this right before the inferno completely consumed the area, destroying everything in its path.

The young male sat as high as he could in the leafy tree and let out a series of high pitch shrieks, hoping they would be heard over the roar of the fire behind him.

Waiting a few moments, he cried out again, remembering the response his mother's own callout had produced just a few days ago. Minutes passed by and there was still no response. Undeterred and with no other option, the ape continued calling out, his shriek becoming louder and stronger each time. While Amelia had not been able to pinpoint their exact position, Pongo felt the shelter mustn't be too far from their home, and therefore close to their family of apes. All he could hope for was that just one of them would acknowledge his call, and he knew the rest would follow.

It seemed like forever before the call finally came back, followed by another, then another as the sound of the forest came to life with a chorus of cries. Beneath him, the group of men immediately stopped what they were doing in response to the noise, and began turning in all directions, trying to establish just where all of these sounds were coming from. But they were everywhere, growing louder by the second as a host of primates moved closer to them, responding to the callout as they quickly travelled toward the shelter.

Pongo stayed where he was, perched in the treetop, repeating his cry until he finally saw movement amongst the trees as a multitude of red bodies approached him.

Don was still standing defiantly with his weapon raised to his face. His body now turning this way and that, looking for an opportunity to take a shot at one of the oncoming creatures. Occasionally he glanced toward his son, aiming his rifle at the pair in the hope the ape would move away from Henry and he could get a clear shot.

All the while, more and more apes continued to descend on the area, arriving from all directions in a spectacular display of unity. A sea of orange bodies was moving through the leafy trees of the gully.

Pongo stood on a branch gesturing for them to come and join him when suddenly his eyes welled up with tears and his breath was taken from him.

Through the trees, a familiar figure was moving towards him, a large bulky frame negotiating the branches and heading slowly in his direction. Overcome with emotion, Pongo could only watch as Marla approached the shelter, her long arms grabbing at the vines that were leading her directly towards the young male.

Immediately the young ape began to wonder if his mother was also nearby and he cast his gaze beyond that of his aunt as he nervously searched through the woodlands.

He needn't have worried as a smooth voice interrupted him and a warm hand gently took hold of his shoulder. The young male turned, his legs buckling on the branch as the smell of his mother instantly filled his nostrils and the familiarity of her touch melted his heart.

Collapsing into her fur laden chest, Pongo breathed a sigh of relief as Rangi wrapped her loving arms around him, bending and smelling the scent from her son's head.

Amelia was overwhelmed as she observed the goings on from her vantage point, relieved to see so many of her kind arriving at the shelter, ready to help rescue the pair.

Still holding the young boy firmly, she watched as Rangi approached her young son, witnessing their emotional reunion as he embraced his mother, tears welling in her own eyes at the display. Looking beyond them, Amelia suddenly spotted Ma, instantly causing the young female's heart to jump with joy.

Without a thought, the excited ape forgot the earlier advice and let go of the young boy, moving quickly toward the edge of the nest. Leaning out of it as far as she was able, Amelia began calling out and signalling to Marla, relieved to see her just a few trees away, happy to know they too would soon be reunited.

The excited shriek instantly caught Don's attention, its exhilarated pitch standing out amongst the din of the forest. Immediately he whisked around, turning in the direction of the nest where his son was trapped. Looking through the haze, he noticed the ape that was with Henry had moved and was now alone, waving its arms erratically in the direction of the shelter.

Don smirked and raised his weapon, quickly training in on the animal. *Got you,* he thought to himself as he slowly cocked the gun and prepared to take his best shot at the creature.

Suddenly a voice broke through Don's concentration. "You will have to shoot me first Mister," the voice proclaimed.

"What did you say?" the frustrated American scowled, as he looked up to find a small man standing directly in front of the rifle, blocking his view of the ape.

"I said you will have to shoot me first," Wayan repeated, holding his ground and refusing to move.

Don's nostrils began flaring with anger as he furiously pushed the nozzle of the gun into the old man's chest in an attempt to shove him to one side.

Unfazed, Wayan quickly repositioned himself, moving back in front of the barrel of the gun, staring defiantly at his boss.

"Mister, the orangutan is the red man of the forest," the elderly man stated. "They come to help your son," he continued, pointing at the creatures around him. "Mister, this is THEIR home," he said, now holding the end of the gun and pressing it against his own chest. "If you shoot them, then you must shoot me first," he repeated, standing defiantly in front of his boss.

Don stared the man down, daring himself to pull the trigger and be done with the foolish old man, his finger quivering with rage over the catch.

"You'll have to shoot me too." A voice came from behind the American as Bayu stepped forward and stood alongside his father. "And me," a second voice added. "Me too," said another, as one by one the men came forward and stood alongside Wayan.

Don angrily pushed the body of the weapon into the chest of the defiant old man, thrusting it forwards with both of his hands. "That's my son!" he screamed, pointing at the child. "These are just apes!" he shouted, pointing around him. Anxiously the father turned to the rest of the men. "My son!" he shouted towards them, his voice breaking down into tears. "He's my son," he repeated as he fell to his knees and began sobbing uncontrollably.

Wayan pointed to two of the men, ordering them to stay with the American and look after him, picking up the discarded weapon that was lying on the ground and slinging it over his own shoulder.

Turning to the others, the elderly man lifted his arm. "Let's go," he commanded, pointing across the water.

"Let's go and get the boy."

Hands through the forest

The fire was now looming a few hundred feet away when the group of men arrived at the shelter. Wayan extended his hand, palm down, to the group of apes, indicating that they were of no threat.

Pointing to his team, then across to Don, the elderly man attempted to explain that there would be no more issues between them. Equally, both parties shared responsibility for the stranded pair; it was time to work together.

Bayu spotted the unusual ape he had seen previously and nodded toward him, acknowledging their association. Pongo returned the gesture to the young man, accepting the truce between them.

With no time to spare, the group started to move toward the location of the trapped couple, the apes moving swiftly through the vines, while the humans travelled cautiously across the ground beneath them.

The heat of the flames was now scorching the arms of both humans and apes while the bark from the trees started to break off ahead of the inferno; causing little cinders to land on the parched forest floor, igniting small pockets of fire here and there.

A small group of men moved away from the main party, taking themselves closer to the edge of the fire where they could quickly slash away lines of foliage, creating breaks that would slow the pace of the inferno down. Others used the large waxy leaves from nearby native plants to beat down the small blazes that were popping up around them.

Amongst the treetops the apes moved swiftly from tree to tree, positioning themselves strategically in place, preparing themselves for the rescue of Amelia and the boy.

At this point, Pongo was just a few vines short of his friend who was clinging onto the frightened child; anxious, but relieved to see the face of her pal, as he moved across the branches between them.

Stopping for a moment, the young male looked downwards, his eyes searching what he could see of the forest floor, hoping to catch sight of his friend; but the smoke was too thick, obscuring his vision. If Sabah was there, it would be impossible to see him.

Glancing back toward the line of apes, Pongo raised his arm to gesture that the rescue was about to begin. He turned back toward Amelia, his face breaking into a huge smile as he prepared to cross the last section between them.

Back at the base, Don was sitting on the hard floor of the forest, his arms extended around his knees and head rested atop of them. He watched as the apes moved swiftly towards his son. Tears streamed down his face, creating streaks of black dirt as the petrified father hoped and prayed that the old man was right about this.

Occasionally he would raise his binoculars and glance towards the boy, his heart breaking at the sight of the small child, trapped alongside a wild animal, flames mercilessly licking at the trees beyond him. It took the man all his might and strength in his soul not to run to the aid of his petrified young son.

Just across from the stranded pair, Bayu was scaling a nearby tree and attempting to communicate with the young child, his voice lost in the commotion. Resorting to basic hand signals, the young supervisor conveyed the message that Henry should not be scared and should do as the apes wanted, that they were here to help him. The young boy responded with a small nod, acknowledging the information before returning his head to the safety of his companion's large fur lined chest as the rescue began to get underway.

Using his powerful frame, Pongo began to rock backwards and forwards, causing the tree he was on to start swaying, the branches bending rhythmically under his weight; bringing him closer to the trapped pair. Continuing this action, the young ape was able to generate enough motion so that he could reach out and grab branches from their tree, finally able to cross the expanse that separated them.

Scrambling into their nest, Pongo immediately took Amelia into his arms. He was so pleased to see her and even happier to be holding her. His emotional embrace was met with a mutual warmth as the young friends reunited.

Glancing at the young boy, Pongo flicked him a little smile and slight wink of the eye before preparing to evacuate them from this increasingly dangerous situation.

Looking up towards his son, Don watched on as a second ape entered the nest where Henry was stuck, his heart beating hard inside his chest with dread, hoping for the best, but fearing the worst.

At the same time, the men that were sitting alongside him stood up, excitedly pointing to the tree line, tapping the anxious father's shoulder and indicating for him to watch.

"Look, look!" they cried out. "Look, look," they continued, their fingers tracing the line of apes that crossed the skyline.

Don reached for his binoculars and stood up, wiping his face with his arm before raising the apparatus to observe the goings on. As far as his eyes could see there was an ape in every tree, creating a magnificent formation that lead from the shelter right across to where his son was trapped.

Pongo gently reached out to the boy, signalling for him to come closer where he could take hold of his small body and help guide him from the nest. Nervously, Henry clambered across the woody structure, taking hold of the ape's waxy long fingers for balance as he began to cross towards him.

As soon as the boy was safely sitting on Pongo's lap, the male ape sat up tall and raised his arm, gesturing to his companions that the rescue would now begin.

It was a spectacular sight that day as one by one the apes moved into action, extending their long orange coloured limbs as far as they were able and reaching their hands through the forest toward each other.

Coupling their fingers together to form a chain, the animals began to pull themselves tighter, slowly bridging the spaces between the trees and forming a ladder of red fur bodies, which Henry could use to climb down to safety.

Back in the nest, Pongo smiled at the young boy, offering him reassurance one last time before carefully lifting the child from the nest and across toward the first tree and on his way to freedom.

Don watched the rescue through his binoculars, the rims of which were now moistened by the tears that were streaming down his face.

Humbled, the American looked on as the group of apes gently guided his son to safety, almost as if he was one of their own. One by one they offered their bulky frames for the boy to climb upon as he slowly disembarked the trees.

Some of the animals let go of the waxy hand behind them, choosing to wrap an arm around the small boy, helping to steady him through the trickier sections, while others let Henry scramble over them, allowing the boy to slide down their lengthy limbs and on towards the next tree.

Below, men cheered as they watched the rescue, amazed as these wild animals saved the boy in spectacular fashion. Mesmerised, they couldn't help but observe the gentle and tender manner the apes held toward the child, until the moment his small body reached the ground, and an instant roar of joy filled the air.

For a moment the abandoned shelter was alive again with activity as apes moved amongst humans, both kinds celebrating the rescue of their own. Henry was sitting on the lap of the supervisor, gulping water down from a canister one of the men had offered him and cramming down some biscuits that Bayu found in his pack.

Meanwhile, Amelia was tucked securely under the strong orange arm of Marla. Completely exhausted, her eyes were so heavy that they would shut for a minute or two as she nuzzled into the warmth of the mother figure's body.

Pongo returned to the safety of his own mother's side, where he relayed the story of the past few days. Sitting alongside her bulky frame, the young ape crammed in whatever food was at hand while telling her in greater detail about the tiger, the humans, the shelter and eventually Sabah, tears beginning to splash on the platform beneath them as he revealed he didn't think he had survived.

Tenderly, Rangi pulled her son closer, reassuring him with a big squeeze; gently reminding him of how he'd just saved Amelia and the human child, and how incredibly proud she was of him.

As the pair sat, recovering from the ordeal, Rangi looked around her, noticing the small child sitting on the lap of a man. *That was maybe his father,* she thought to herself, observing their likeness. Glancing beyond them she noticed an older man, his weathered and wise face familiar to her. He was like one of the many humans she'd seen through her years, natives of the forest themselves; immediately sensing that he was a good man, a gentle soul that could be trusted.

Then, across the water, the female ape caught sight of a lone figure, an unusual looking man sitting by himself, neither celebrating nor sharing the moment with anyone. Puzzled, the female continued watching him, trying to understand who or what he was in this situation.

Don looked up as the feeling that he was being watched came over him. Instantly, his eyes met the gaze of the large female orangutan who was sitting on the platform nursing the ape that had saved Henry. Trying to muster up a smile, the father half tilted his head at the creature, nodding awkwardly in her direction, attempting to offer some form of acknowledgement. The female ape did not return the gesture. Instead, she protectively pulled her son a little tighter to her chest; sensing that, without doubt, this was the human her kind should fear.

Mother and son sat together for a few moments longer before deciding to leave the shelter for a safer location. The fire was still quickly heading towards them and would soon take hold of the abandoned buildings, its old dry frame providing the perfect elements for the hungry flames to consume.

Pongo raised himself to his feet and quickly lumbered across to Amelia who was preparing to leave also, wanting to see her one last time before they departed. Greeting the young female, the youngster lowered his head in shame and raised his finger to her eye, hoping that she would forgive him. Instead, Amelia took his hand and moved it towards her mouth, pursing her lips together, she lightly kissed the end of his finger.

Suddenly, their moment was disturbed as Henry hurried toward them, throwing his arms around the pair while burying his head into Amelia's furry coat. The child stood there for a minute, holding them both like he wouldn't let go, as Bayu remained close to him preparing for the party to leave. Pongo glanced across toward the man, nodding his head in acknowledgment, the supervisor immediately returning his gesture with a respectful bow and polite smile before motioning to the child to leave.

Stopping suddenly, the small boy turned and reached up to the apes, pursing his lips and touching them lightly on their cheeks, giving them both a kiss goodbye. Pongo looked quickly toward Amelia and back at the child. Knowingly he smiled and flushed, realising this was 'I love you' in the language of the humans.

Soon the shelter had fallen back into silence, the hive of activity was finished as both humans and apes went their own way, each party heading back to the safety of their homes.

Tall flames were now visible as they reached into the night sky, creating a glorious back drop of orange and gold, dancing higher and higher as it edged closer towards the empty buildings.

Amelia took one last look at the shelter before departing the area, glancing across at the buildings that she had once called home, a place that was very special in her heart. Taking it all in, the female looked across towards the tree where she and Henry had been trapped. It had already gone, flames consuming it a short time ago, leaving just a dark empty void in its place.

Quietly, the female ape said her farewells as she prepared to move through the vines and away from this place forever, tears beginning to spill down her cheeks.

Stopping, Amelia glanced back for one last look, her thoughts immediately turning to the friend she was leaving behind.

"Goodbye Sabah," she whispered into the empty gully. "Goodbye my beautiful friend."

A debt has to be repaid

The journey back to the worksite was relatively quick, the men retracing the same route they'd created in the initial stages of the search.

Henry spent his time perched atop of Bayu's shoulders, his tired body slumped wearily over the small man's frame as they travelled together through the woodland.

Now and again the boy's eyes would close, the rhythmic motion of the supervisor's movements lulling him gently to sleep, only rousing when the terrain became a little tougher, and caused the small boy to stir.

Don was walking ahead of the party on his own, silently contemplating what had just occurred, his head hung low as thoughts of what could have been ran through his mind, while relieved that the outcome had turned out as it did.

Reaching the edge of the site, an excited Vania ran toward the group, screaming out her son's name. She raced through the scrub toward the child who now stood alongside his father. Picking him up, the mother span him around, kissing the small boy's dirty face while rustling his hair with her hands, holding his tiny body as hard as she was able.

Don stood back and watched as his wife preened their child, checking his small frame for injuries while repeatedly kissing the top of his head.

As he watched their interaction he was immediately reminded of the mother ape he had seen across the water, reuniting with her own son, similarly sharing the same affectionate mannerisms.

Instantly the guilty father felt a sense of shame come over him and he quickly turned away from the pair, hurriedly moving towards the cabin, trying to push the thoughts from his mind as he entered the small wooden building.

Slowly the workplace cleared out as the tired, but relieved men bid their farewells to each other, one by one leaving the site for the comfort of their own homes. Henry had already left with his mother, his father lifting his tired and sleepy body into the back of the black vehicle, deciding to follow the pair home a little later.

Bayu kindly offered to stay on with his boss and keep him company, concerned that the man was being unusually quiet and maybe required a little bit of support. Thanking the young man, and grateful for his offer, Don reassured him that he was just tired, telling his supervisor to leave him there and take his elderly father, Wayan, home.

With everyone gone, Don now sat on the steps of the cabin, completely alone and glad to have a moment to himself.

Running his hand through his mop of dark hair, the man looked up, noticing the twinkling stars pinned neatly against the black backdrop of the night sky. He sighed, resting his arms on his knees as his thoughts turned to the female ape that he'd seen across the water.

Replaying the moment in his mind, the swarthy American could see the way she looked at him. He shuddered, it was a look of complete revulsion as she tucked her young son further into her body.

Standing up, the man kicked at the loose stones that covered the dusty ground, while looking out to the darkness of the forest, wondering just how an animal managed to make him feel this way.

Conflicted, the father moved around the grounds, contemplating how he could make this right; his troubled soul knowing that he was indebted to the apes that had saved his son.

Moving back inside the building, the businessman sat down at his desk and opened his computer, searching page after page for images of the apes, hoping to find the face of the kind that had saved Henry's life. If he did then maybe he could donate some money to a charity.

However as the hours ticked by, Don became more and more intrigued with the information he read as he discovered the species that he'd seen, Pongo Pygmaeus, were in fact so rare they would soon die out. Further, the shelters, like the one they came across, were abandoned, not because men like him had bought the land they were on, but because there were fewer and fewer apes able to be saved as their species had declined so much.

From time to time Don would sit back and rub his stubbly chin with his hands, his mind dancing from one idea to another as he stared at the images on the screen. In Henry's future these creatures would not exist, and shamefully he would be partly responsible. Occasionally the man would go outside for a breath of fresh air, the solitary cries of creatures in the night catching his attention; reflecting on what it would be like here with no sound at all.

That night was one of the longest in Don's life as gratitude for his son's survival gave way to the feelings of guilt and shame the female ape had brought upon him.

Doodling haphazardly, the businessman looked down to the piece of paper he'd been scribbling on, smiling at the amateur image of the Pongo ape he'd drawn.

Circling the image, Don sat back in his chair, his heart beginning to beat a little faster as an idea began to take shape in his mind.

It was at that moment he knew that he could keep the site; that the workers, Bayu and his father Wayan, could keep their jobs, and Henry's legacy would still exist. In fact, he thought to himself, it would be even greater.

Scribbling two words above and below the circled image, Don sat back and smiled at the logo, the face of the ape that saved his son staring back as Project Pongo was born.

The years that passed saw Don's plant size grow by thousands of hectares, the logo that now branded all of his products generating more income than he could have dreamed of; allowing him to buy vast areas of land; farming some, while leaving most as jungle.

His son Henry, now grown, had studied conservation, his experience with Amelia and the apes had shaped his life in a way he could not have imagined. Henry did go on to work for his father, and this had become his legacy, but not in the way that they expected all those years ago.

Henry had become caretaker of his native land, looking after the jungle that remained untouched.

While he disagreed with any destruction of this land, Henry knew palm oil was too popular a product these days, finding its way into everyday items and to every corner of the world. The young man was well aware that if his father didn't own this land, then someone else would, and without doubt it would have been destroyed long ago.

Daily, the handsome young man would drive the tracks of the forest in his jeep with his old friend Bayu sitting alongside him, ensuring the area was safe and free from illegal activities and the fires had not spilled over their boundaries.

From time to time the pair would stop as they spotted a family of apes sitting high in the trees, peacefully living their lives in the warmth of the sun. Watching them, the two men would reminisce about that night, happy to see their old friends once again.

Pongo was now fully grown, his appearance quite changed, with large flanges that now framed his face and a bulky masculine body. Ever watchful, the male ape would gesture to Amelia when a vehicle approached. She would glance down to see the two men looking up at them. Always, the female ape would stop what she was doing and smile for a moment. Her time with the boy, stranded together was never forgotten, her heart instantly warming at the sight of the grown up young man beneath her.

"Look," she called out to her offspring as she pointed to the forest floor.

"Look, our human friend has come to visit," she continued, motioning to the energetic boy.

Pongo glanced across at his son who was busy twirling sticks through his toes, playing in the leafy green forest. Stopping for a second, the lively youngster looked down toward the men in the vehicle and half smiled. The story of the fire, the human boy and his uncle, was a familiar tale his parents had relayed to him many a time.

But the young ape was easily distracted and would quickly return to what he was doing, completing some somersaults before landing in a nearby nest, the sound of his parents laughter filling the air.

As always, the vehicle would depart and leave the forest to return to its natural chatter as birds and bees darted from tree to tree and animals crunched over the ground below.

The youngster would lay quietly chewing on his bark and looking up toward the blue sky, watching as the branches of the treetops danced in and out of his view. Settling into his cosy nest, with the security of his parents nearby, young Sabah would finally succumb to the warmth of the afternoon sun and the overwhelming urge to close his eyes, once again falling asleep peacefully in his beautiful rainforest home.

The End

Acknowledgements

While Pongo is a fictional story, the plight for orangutans is very real; they are identified as critically endangered by the World Wildlife Fund. Sadly, the Sumatran Orangutans are likely to be extinct within 10 years; the Bornean Orangutans like Pongo, soon after. The very thought of my grandchildren growing up to only see this gentle species within the confines of a zoo compelled me to write the book. What better way to raise awareness than to write a story?

Orangutans are part of the ape family, residing only in South East Asia and share 98% of their DNA with humans. With four fingers and opposable thumbs they are the most like us in the primate kingdom.

Did you know that in Malay, the word orang means human while the word hutan means forest, so orang-hutan actually means person of the forest. I find it easy to believe that in years gone past, both humans, like Wayan, and orangutans lived harmoniously together within the leafy green forests of Borneo and Sumatra.

So, what has changed since then? Deforestation of these vast jungles has occurred to make way for palm oil plants which produce an oil found in many everyday products - from shampoo to pizza dough, lipstick to instant noodles. Palm oil is an extremely popular product to use as it is cheap and can be found in more than half of your supermarket products. However, without reading the contents of each and every item you purchase, palm oil can be easily overlooked and quickly forgotten.

Identification of products, like Don's *Project Pongo* logo, do exist and make it easier for consumers to make informed choices. Through labelling - such as 'palm oil free', or 'sustainable palm oil' we can identify what we should be purchasing. Please go to our website, https://www.hellopongo.com for more information on what logos to look for when you go shopping.

Unfortunately, the decline of the orangutan is a man-made problem, and only by raising awareness and changing how we shop can we undo it. Remembering that each time we purchase a product with palm oil in it, an ape - be it mother, child or Pongo, just lost their home.

Environmental awareness and learning about sustainable development are a serious aspect of the book as we travel into Pongo's world, meet delightful characters, see the destruction caused by the palm oil industry and discover the importance of looking after the environment and wildlife.

There are so many people to thank for helping me finish this book; from dear friends who patiently read through it in its infant form, to family who sat at the dinner table listening to a chapter and giving input as to how the book could evolve. A special thank you to my daughter Siobhan for her stunning illustration of Pongo. They say it takes a village to raise a child... well my village created Pongo, hopefully we can make a difference.

Oddly I have to thank my back...you see, it was my back giving way that brought me to writing the book. As a former fitness instructor, being bedridden for months on end could have caused me to go crazy; days of endless monotony and boredom could have taken me down a different path entirely. However, it made me assess my purpose, realising that although my body didn't work, my mind did. So before, during and after major surgery, I was able to disappear for hours on end to the jungles of Borneo and bring Pongo to life. I have looked back on that traumatic time with much fondness as I wondered just who did Pongo save? Was it Henry or was it myself?

I have to acknowledge my dogs, who sat patiently alongside me through the journey, whose eyes I looked into for inspiration on how I thought an animal would think. My Prince, who didn't complete the journey and who now lives in our hearts.

Mostly and always, I have to thank my husband and soulmate Will, who lifted me up (literally and emotionally) and carried me through that time. Who encouraged me each day to write and listened to each and every word as it evolved. The man who has never read a book in his life helped me write this one.

Not everyone can write a book, and I certainly didn't think I could either; but I did and I'm proud.

Thank you for reading it,
I hope you enjoyed the story.

Sue

Author Bio

Sue Feenstra is a 49 year old mother, wife and animal lover.

Originally from Hereford, England, Sue worked as a fitness instructor in many gyms across her hometown. After leaving the United Kingdom in 1998, Sue continued her career in New Zealand before settling on the Gold Coast, Australia.

However, after years of heavy exercise, her back began to suffer, forcing her to give up her active life, and ultimately, leaving her bed-bound for months at a time.

With nothing to do, and determined to not let it get her down, Sue's thoughts turned to those less fortunate. There, while bed-ridden for months, Sue discovered the plight of the Orangutan's in South East

Asia. After much research, she felt compelled to write a book and raise awareness for the destructive deforestation necessary for the production of palm oil.

'Pongo' is Sue's first book, a fictional story about a lively young ape, facing the devastating destruction of his home. Written in breath-taking detail, Pongo transports you to the jungles of Borneo, shares a wonderful insight into the lives of this gentle species, and considers the consequences of deforestation on our wildlife.

Sue is also the creator of **Hello Pongo**, a brand that aims to stop deforestation by raising funds for associated organisations through its range of palm oil free products.

After undergoing major back surgery in 2017, Sue is now up and about, and back to her energetic self. But with a different outlook on life! With three young grandchildren, Sue's passion has shifted from making people healthier, to making the world healthier. With the support of her husband and children, Sue plans to write more books that highlight the need for awareness and ultimately, change; so our future generations have a legacy left to enjoy.

ORANGUTAN FOUNDATION
INTERNATIONAL
AUSTRALIA

Orangutan Foundation International Australia's (OFIA) mission is to support and continue the orangutan and forest conservation efforts initiated by Dr Biruté Mary Galdikas in Kalimantan, Borneo. Dr Galdikas, who is Patron and a Board Member of OFIA, is an internationally renowned environmentalist, anthropologist and the world's foremost orangutan expert.

OFIA has two core campaigns; caring for orphaned and displaced orangutans at the OFI Care Centre & Quarantine in Pasir Panjang Village, Central Kalimantan, Indonesian Borneo; and, securing habitat for their future release.

OFI currently care for 330+ orangutans at their Care Centre. These orangutans have been orphaned due to the destruction of their habitat for palm oil plantations, illegal logging & mining. Without the OFI Care Centre, these beautiful, gentle apes would be homeless and more than likely dead. The Care Centre is a half-way house for orangutans, providing them with food, shelter and love along with the skills they will need when they are old enough to be released back into the wild.

However, for that eventual release to be successful, land needs to be secured to ensure they have a safe place to live.

Through The Orangutan Legacy Forest project, OFI purchases, protects and replants forest habitat in Borneo that is vital to the orangutan's survival - land which is protected from poachers, palm oil plantations, illegal loggers and miners, creating a large, protected and interconnected orangutan habitat 'sanctuary', keeping wild orangutans safe and creating this much needed sanctuary for the release of rehabilitated orangutans from the Care Centre. With so little protected forest remaining, and with many national parks off limits to ex-captive animals, this initiative offers a real and tangible future for those animals once they are ready to return to the wild.

For the orangutans currently being cared for by OFI, the Orangutan Legacy Forest truly is 'the promised land.' Each month more orangutans arrive at the Care Centre where they enter OFI's rehabilitation program.

You can foster one of our beautiful orangutan infants. As a foster parent, you will be helping care for the displaced and orphaned orangutans at the OFI Care Centre, contributing to the medical, dietary and emotional care that the orangutans need to thrive during their rehabilitation back to the wild. To foster an orangutan, go to our website http://orangutanfoundation.org.au/orangutan/become-a-foster-parent/

For more information about Orangutan Foundation International Australia, or to donate, please visit our website.

Website: www.orangutanfoundation.org.au
Email: info@ofiaustralia.com
Phone: 61 7 5527 5226
Facebook: OrangutanFoundationInternationalAustralia
Instagram: ofi_australia
Twitter: twitter.com/DrBirute